AF596085

It comes in threes

A story for her…

Seanokeng J.

synopsis

Patrick N. Mot - a thirteen year old seventh grader with an over active imagination living under the warmth of both parents is plunged into reality when his mother dies, and not so long subsequent to her diagnosis at the local children's hospital where she worked as a nurse.
Just towards the end of the year that saw the passing of a mother, a wife, and the most decorated nurse Roseville has ever had, the father disappears without a trace, leaving young Patrick to deal with reality all by his lonesome self. But the youngster had a different plan of action; instead of dealing with reality, he intended to defy it.

A week after the passing of his mother he had asked his questions to his Sciences teacher who played the role of mentor and friend. Patrick asked all there was to know about death till he ultimately decided that he did not want to suffer the same fate as everything else that is or once was alive.
He worked tirelessly in his mentor's house laboratory during that year of his seventh grade with hopes of finding a path to that grey area between life and death, a prolonged lifespan.

After taking refuge in his mentor's house who got arrested for tax evasions the youngster begins a rather solitary journey filled with blood spattering experiments trying to perfect one of the two procedures in his two self-formulated theories.
Patrick had everything planned out, every step mapped up, but that's not how life works. He never factored in falling in love or the risk that comes with it; the loss of those he held dear to himself just as his father had warned him.
The pressure to perfect his farfetched idea is elevated when he has to use it to save his mentor who has played the role of a father to him. And he would have no one else but the love of his life as he makes this desperate attempt to save Alfred's life...

Chapter Summary

CHAPTER **Page**

CHAPTER ONE: The plunge

The lab works and preparations for Alfred's resurrection were at long last complete. And with the compatible substitute body acquired, at the least, Patrick deserved his eight hour sleep for the first time in two months. But circumstance would not let the young doctor have it.

Just at the crack of dawn, no more than three hours into his sleep, the young nurse he worked with had to come rushing into the house for him.

Hannah slept in her home just across the street, but she made sure that every sunrise she'd walk over to Mr. T's to assess the dying man's condition, and go on to give a report to Patrick in the house, sometimes over joint breakfast.

On his bedroom door she banged loudly and screamed out his name. Yet got no answer back, and when she tested the door, it was locked from the inside. It meant he was in there, and not in the lab, like on most mornings. She could only keep banging and calling out his name with hope that her frail voice at the aid of the bangs would pull him from his slumber.

At only a minute's length Patrick finally came to the door and opened it, but his eyes woke to a sad face flooded with heavy tears. She stepped forward and let herself fall into his bare chest, wrapped her arms around him with a heavy but gentle squeeze.

Patrick was confused as he was surprised, his mouth that close to her ear he asked "What's wrong, love?" but when Hannah looked up into his eyes she couldn't bring herself to it, saying it to him. She could not be the one to tell him the only words that she knew would surely break him, she just couldn't.

After a while trying to calm her down and stop the tears that kept flowing while trying to figure out why she was so sad, he slowly began to see it, just as one would the warm gleaming light from the sun that had been hidden under dark heavy clouds for far too long. The tears were not hers, they were his! She was crying on his behalf.

He held her softly by the shoulders. And when she looked again up into his eyes, Patrick straightened his brow, his eyes widened and he asked with a stutter "Is it... is it Alfred?"The chokes in his voice, she had not said anything, yet he was already shattering.

"I'm sorry!" She said amid her tears, and that's all she said, all she could

say really, but it was enough, enough to set him on a rollercoaster of emotions he's never felt the likes of before. He panted heavily for air, and felt himself lose the battle to stand up straight, any moment he would fall down to his knees, it felt. Sounds disappeared. When he'd look away from her reddened teary eyes everything around him was slowly but surely in his eyes spinning and bending out of shape.
He thought he'd pass out, he hoped to pass out, or at the least wake up on his bed from the nightmare, but he wouldn't, because this was no dream, the moment was as real as it gets. It was the clear and total real manifestation of his worst fear, death, mortality!
And all of the sudden, there it was! The extreme and uncontrollable need to see Alfred, yet he dreaded what he'd see when he gets there. His body told him to step back to take a sit on the bed or even lay back in it, but no, all he wanted was to see his mentor. Stumbling round her he walked out the bedroom barefooted and bare-chested still with only the shorts he always slept in on.
Hannah hesitantly followed after him, walking slowly behind him and unable to stop the loop that played on and on in her head.
That sunrise on her morning routine check-up on Mr. T, she found him not breathing and noticed that the machine that measured his vitals was no longer beeping as it should. Questioning the machines she went on to check the man's vitals herself, the old manual way. With her index finger along with the middle finger she searched for a pulse, and she still reached the same conclusion as the machine.
Mr. Alfred Maoto Tobetsa, Patrick's friend, former primary school teacher, mentor and most of all; father-figure, was no more. He was dead!
His face distorted by the painfully devastating realization Patrick stood looking down at the dead body of Alfred, but his tears, they would not flow, not just yet.

Hesitant at it Hannah finally walked in, and stood closely behind Patrick, who seemed rather collected, shockingly collected.
It was completely silent in the room. Alfred lay dead on the bed and Patrick stood above him like a statue, so much silence with zero movement like the moment itself had frozen in time entirely. Not knowing what to do or say, she just stood there shivering from the nonexistent cold, hoping that Patrick would show some emotion, that maybe that would prompt her of what she was to do next, force any of her natural responses.

And just as the silence and unemotional response started to become concerning to the nurse, it began!
That close to him she could hear his heavy breathing, and just when he would seem to fall to his knees, she quickly caught him only to let him down slowly. Overwhelmed by the vertigo he held on to the floor and the desperate struggle for air continued. "Hannah! I can't breathe, I can't...I can't breathe!" he said repeatedly clutching his right chest just above where the heart would be. "What's happening to me?" he asked, and with the shock in his voice she could tell that whatever he was feeling he was feeling for the very first time in his life. His heart has never broken before.
"Your heart is breaking." She replied kneeling beside him and turned slightly to pull him gently to herself, "It's pain you're feeling. It will do you no good holding it inside, it's okay to let it out." and like that the bellowing accompanied by streams of tears began and would transition into screams at the top of his lungs. He screamed in cries his mentor's name, begging him to return to the living, begging him to return to him even if it was for a moment to at the least say 'thank you' and even 'goodbye' to those wise fatherly eyes.
Never letting go she held on to him, and that's all she could do for him really, hold him tightly and never let go as his heart broke apart.

Minutes passed and the crying stopped, but to her it had felt to have lasted an eternity. With shimmering wet eyes he looked steadily into hers, "Tell me I made him proud." And at that moment it seemed the right response from her would heal his broken heart or at the least pull the pieces back together and let father time do the rest, mend it.
Her forehead against his and hands on his cheeks she replied truthfully mentioning how Patrick was all Alfred ever spoke of, bragged about even. "And if that's not enough, Patrick, you still have your whole life ahead of you to make him even more proud." She added. And when he would ask her to leave him alone with Alfred and to not call the hearse for the corpse's collection just yet, she would not argue, feeling he deserved all the time he needed to accept what was and let go. She for one knows the dire importance of accepting loss and letting go, three suicide attempts following her own mother's demise...

...But this too, like every tale, deserves to be told from the beginning, from moments before the plunge. Before this young doctor ever even considered being a doctor himself, so let's go there, together, to the beginning of his story...

Younger Patrick Mot reached for the door and twisted the knob. But when he took his first step beyond the door line, his foot wouldn't find the floor.
By the time he realized that he was dreaming, it was too late, for he was then falling off his bed. A splitting curse cracked the air. But being an active person, he stood up as soon as he fell to the near hard floor below.
Patrick, a thirteen year old seventh grader turning fourteen in that year's August. He has had the predicament of sleep walking since the age of five. It was only by a miracle that no severe injury had come out of it up to then. His parents on the other hand, did not see his sleep walking as a problem, but rather as proof, the evidence that indeed young Patrick had an over-active imagination.
After tending to his tender left shoulder he put on his PJs - he had a vast variety of PJs to choose from, but rarely put them on at night when he slept. He chose the blue PJs with his favorite action figure printed on them - Beastboy - and barefooted he headed for the bedroom door, for real this time.
As he opened the white door to make his way to the kitchen, where breakfast would be served, he bumped into his father - Mr. Mot - whom too had just woken up and had come to wake Patrick up. John Mot was an older version of his only son Patrick - same eye color, same nose shapes, dark complexions, the only differences were the sizes and the heights, the voices as well, John Mot's was deeper and bolder.

The two made their way along the thin passageway inside the seven roomed house with grey painted inner walls while pushing and grabbing one another as the men in wrestling did. And once again Mrs. Mot, Patrick's mother, had to play the referee to stop them. It was not like the two times high school beauty pageant winner had the muscle power to stop any of the two. Alice Mot was not a woman of a big stature. What she lacked in physical strength she made up for in the verbal power to stop both of them. And stop them she did, "Would the two of you stop that! The porridge is getting cold!" she raised her voice to a tone both Patrick and his father preferred to go a day or two without hearing, but that with how the two tended to interact; was close to impossible to achieve.

A rather happy family of three, designated in the outskirt of the North province, in a little middleclass residential area named Roseville. Roseville was a black dominated town, and it was all 'thanks' to the law

enforced race division of the unforgettable apartheid era. But the town was far developed than most of the other known black dominated towns, which resulted in a fair number of other races moving into the town in the early 2000s, mostly for employment and business ventures. And two new schools, a primary and a secondary school, had to be constructed just outside the town to cater for the irruption in the population.
Patrick was growing under the tenderness and placate of both parents whom even at his age at times for being the only child had the propensity to treat like a toddler, and could've most likely contributed to his antisocial demeanor.
Apart from his parents; his Sciences' teacher was the only friend he had, but that did not create a life of early boredom for young Patrick. His parents after learning of his behavior to not interact with others on a level of making friends, did their best to get him the best and even costly home entertainment equipments on the market.

His parents were high school sweethearts who married and relocated to Roseville just a year prior to the birth of their first and only child, Patrick of course. Even over fourteen years of marriage their relationship still had that spark! Once or twice every month they went out, just the two of them leaving Patrick in the house with a sitter. The couple would go to the local theater to watch the weekly plays or go to those restaurants that stayed open till very late, and would appreciate one another's company over a meal like a couple that had just started out. It would be fair to correct that their affiliation didn't have 'that spark' but rather the whole flame still...

Patrick and Mr. Mot stopped pushing one another and approached in silence the kitchen table where the soft porridge breakfast had been set.
Mrs. Mot's soft porridge! She turned a mere soft porridge meal into one both Patrick and his father looked forward to having every morning without complaints of having a repetitious meal.
Even the aroma of her porridge and the yellow color though prepared from white maize meal would dare and equally attract even the critics to try it out. And her main secret ingredient, butter!

Before any of the two could take a proper seat before the steaming porridge, Alice Mot had to once again use the '*glare*'. "What are you trying to do?" her voice was a warning and the glare; a persuader's

double headed axe.
"Trying to eat our porridge..." Patrick replied with chokes of doubt in his voice, "It's getting cold, isn't it?" he ended without looking into his mom's searching eyes as to not give away to what he and his dad were doing yet again.
John Mot couldn't wait to add on. "Yeah...we're starving." He said "We haven't eaten since last night." He too did not look his wife directly in the eyes, and for the very same reason as his son wouldn't.
Mrs. Mot asked again, still with a stare at the boys "Have you done the first thing you are supposed to do every morning?" She was then walking closer to the table, probably to sit before her own bowl of warm porridge.

Then both boys replied at once "Yep!" deep down she could already see through it, after all she has had countless encounter with it.
"Which is?" asked the mother with an easier look at the two then, what clever response they had for her this time, she wondered.
"Waking up, of course!" replied both the son and the father again at once, it was these synced responses that gave away their mischievous intends.
"Just go wash up your faces." Mrs. Mot ordered with a smile at the two as she was all caught up to what they were doing yet again.
"Okay mom." Patrick affirmed and walked away from the table, his father followed.
The two enjoyed doing that every morning - teasing the outnumbered woman that is. But the parents had been planning to parent another child and Mrs. Mot had been hoping that it would be a girl this time, for two reasons - helping with the house chores which she did on her own and helping with managing the boys - even she admitted that the two at times could be a lot for a single person to mother and wife. They tended to act way low of their individual ages; her husband like an adolescent teenager and her son like a toddler, which they both weren't.

Minutes past, Mrs. Mot started hearing their bickering getting louder and closer - they were coming back into the kitchen. She knew that she better prepare herself to stop the bickering, or it would get physical again and they would break another one of her striking vases, by accident. She had lost three already.
As soon as the two appeared walking side by side from the corridor she yelled, "Stop it you two or I will "

Patrick and his father approached the table set in the center of the kitchen in mute mode. Each pulled a table chair and seated still with their mouths devoid of a single word's utterance; it was only their eyes that darted around, till finally they were fixed upon the porridge bowls set before them.
It is a way of showing table manners to not speak while eating, so the only sound during that breakfast was that of spoons scooping porridge from the bowls.

Minutes after the breakfast, after Mrs. Mot had tidied up the kitchen she began preparing for her midday shift.
The thirty nine year old mother and wife worked as a nurse at the local hospital - ST. MAPS THE NEILA CHILDREN'S HOSPITAL - it was a little over two kilometers from where the Mot family lived.
Saturdays due to Mrs. Mot's absence at the house during the day were the only days that Patrick and his dad got to have fun without having to worry about Mrs. Mot cutting it short. On weekdays Patrick would be at school and Mr. Mot would be at work wherever that was.
The information of his occupation up to then had never been made clear to young Patrick. For some reason the parents purposely kept it away from him. What harm could it do? Knowing what your father does during the day?
Even at school Patrick wrote his essays on his mother's job again and again for every career day since elementary grades.
On Sundays they couldn't have as much fun as they did on Saturdays because Mrs. Mot didn't work on Sundays. All three would be at home if the day had not been reserved for a little family trip.

John Mot decided to rent video games from the Roseville's own MR. VIDEO store. Both he and his son loved playing video games, and most of the times as adversaries. They used one of the two cars they owned to drive to the store and were back within thirty minutes - Mrs. Mot had gone to work with the other car. They owned only two, and had they had the necessity to buy a third; they would've done so without the hesitation of thinking about going out of the budget. Mrs. Mot got into medical nursing, and children nursing specifically for the love of children, so she didn't mind being underpaid by the local public children's hospital. But whatever job Mr. Mot had on the other hand compared to his wife's; it paid well, great even...

When Mrs. Mot knocked off from work it was six in the evening. The two were too fast asleep in Patrick's room after the home-works that the father oversaw the completion of. So out of it to even hear the car as it drove in.

Mrs. Mot parked the car back into the garage and slowly approached the front door. When she entered her house, she couldn't recognize it as the house she left when she was going to work earlier that day - the two had turned the living room upside down. Junk food containers everywhere and the couches moved from their usual positions. One of the couches - the brown three sitter couch, was pulled really close to the wide and flat television screen. It must have been where they found most comfort when playing their video games. They had really made a mess of the living room.

They did map to shipshape the room before 'their mother' knocked off from work, but cleaning doesn't follow after playing video games for hours and eating more than enough junk food - only sleeping does.

Mrs. Mot knew very well that trying to envisage what was going on in her house during her absence would only give her a mental meltdown. So, the rather disappointed woman went to take a warm bath and went straight to bed after - not to rest but to rather take a deep sleep that not even the quake of the whole earth would wake her from. She didn't even think of the whereabouts of the two individual whom completed her family circle, or rather 'family triangle' given the number of people who completed it.

After just two hours of Mrs. Mot's arrival Mr. Mot woke from Patrick's bedroom and realized that his wife had come back home and was sleeping in their bedroom. So, to postpone being yelled at for acting like a child, he decided to sleep in his son's room - they shared the bed.

Sunday, just at the crack of dawn, Mrs. Mot woke and tidied the mess that Patrick and his father had made the previous day.

Everything was unfolding just as customary - Mrs. Mot prepared her 'famous' soft porridge for breakfast, she had shared the recipe with most of her lady colleagues at work. She even suggested it to many of her patients' parents, and they would come back the next day praising it, telling her how their kids loved it. Seems she didn't keep her secret ingredient 'secret'.

The father and son a while later appeared from the passage that led from Patrick's bedroom with their voices raised high at each other, engaged in the usual bickering. Then the unusual never seen before

started to happen.
Mrs. Mot didn't try to stop them like she usually did. What struck Patrick and his father as even more atypical was that Mrs. Mot didn't tell them to go wash their faces like she usually did. All she did was pace around the kitchen in silence touching this and that. After Patrick had greeted and Mr. Mot had kissed her 'good morning' the two went to the bathroom on their own without Mrs. Mot shouting it at them like she usually had to.

When the two came back into the kitchen Mrs. Mot was still acting somewhat eccentric - she seemed lost in the depths of her own thoughts not paying much attention to anything or anyone around her. John thought that she was like that because of the state she found her living room in yesterday, and Patrick thought so too when he cracked a joke and she didn't even smile.
"Honey, we're both sorry about yesterday…" The father began apologizing "We were going to clean it up. I promise you it will never happen again, right Patrick?"
"Yeah mom, it will never happen again, we promise." The son apologized as well "I mean messing up will never happen again, playing video games…that we can't promise not doing again." He added so with a smile.
"Yes boys, I believe you." murmured Mrs. Mot, while nodding with a forced smile that only the husband could see through.
John Mot knew right away after the apology that yesterday's mess was not the basis of his wife's peculiar silence - something else was eating at her, and he couldn't let it pass just like that.

After the breakfast that even the son could sense that something was off; in an attempt to find out what was going on with his wife, Mr. Mot gave his identification card to Patrick and a fifty rand note. He asked Patrick to return the video games they had rented yesterday back to MR. VIDEO store, thus giving himself time to speak more privately to his wife.
Patrick on the other hand saw this as an opening to trial the speed limits of his new BMX bike. The bike he got from his dad to substitute the one that had been stolen not so long ago when he was visiting his mentor, teacher and friend, Alfred.
The youngster secretly thanked the thieves whoever they were for stealing his old bike, as he had always wanted a new one to replace the one he's had for three long years, though it was not in bad condition.

He knew how to take care of it.
Out the garage Patrick pushed his still shining blue BMX bike - it came with a helmet and knee caps as well as elbow caps - but he never put those on, regardless how many times his mother stressed that he had to.
Alice peaked out the window concerned of her son's safety - she knew how fast Patrick liked to go on that bike. John felt the same way yet he reassured, "He'll be okay, he's a big boy now. Our big boy!" and immediately asked pulling his wife gently back to the couch, "Now tell me what's going on love, what's wrong? I can see that something is weighing you down." To discourage her from falsifying her response he looked her directly in the eyes, a trick that had always been effective on her, he thought.

Alice Mot gazed back at her husband with eyes filling up with tears of sorrow and forced a smile still, "You know me so well, don't you?" she began holding on to his hands, "Yesterday at work during my lunch break I took a blood test to check my fertility levels again and..." She stopped and immediately the tears began racing down to her chin, she clasped on to his hands tighter.
"I'm sorry honey, but we still have a plan 'B'." Mr. Mot comforted the crying woman, "Seanokeng loves us, we love her, she's gonna make a perfect addition to the family. And Pete has agreed to meet her." he added thinking his wife was sad because yesterday she found out that she was somehow no longer viable to mother through natural pregnancy another child. Something they have always feared given the complications that came with her first pregnancy when they almost lost Patrick, their 'Pete', before he was even born into this world. 'The miracle baby' they would regard him in the first six months of his life after he was born prematurely with the unlikeliest chances to survive. But that was not it, her fertility was still intact. But she was ill, very ill. The doctor who had diagnosed her with the terminal illness from the blood test told her that she was carrying a rare virus, one that the modern-day medical world had not yet found a treatment for, let alone an effective cure to. She relayed the devastating news to him.
She couldn't stop crying, and John knew he couldn't stop her even if he tried. When she spoke; it got even sadder. "John, I'll never see him grow up. I won't get to see his first girlfriend..." the list of the things she'd not live to see went on.
It was really saddening to a point that Mr. Mot couldn't hold his own

back - they were both in tears in each other's arms. But John like a man cried in silence, yet felt the pains of his wife to their fullest extends.

The diagnosis estimated with the rate of the spread of the virus within her that she only had two more to live, and no, not years, months! What pained Mrs. Mot more was not that she only had two more months with her son, but that her son only had two more months with his mom. Those tears they shed in each other's arms were not for her, but for him, Patrick, he'd have to grow up without his mother.
Mr. Mot knew firsthand what death of a parent could do to a young boy. He lost both parents one after the other following a car accident that wasn't even remotely their fault. And it would have had scarred him for life had he not met young Alice in high school. But even by then the damage had been done.
Juvenile John Mot was plunged into a reality where death was the cruel enemy, and like any enemy he believed that if he dedicated himself to it enough he could defeat it. Hence the secret day job.
Mr. Mot was working in a research facility dedicated to erasing that one fatal flaw, mortality! He was the lead research scientist in that facility, and has been since its initiation. After all, he was the one who came up with that idea of curing mortality, and at a young age too. He was only nineteen when he put on for the first time his lab coat. And it became the parent's joint decision to keep that other half of John's life a secret from Patrick. John had explained fully to Alice why it was to be so and she agreed as she saw reason the way he did.
But that wasn't going to be the only thing to be kept from Patrick's ears from then on. His mother's sickness too he would not know of, they will not tell.
The couple had to hope for the best and prepare for the inevitable worst to come, death!
Mrs. Mot stood up and went to Patrick's room to see if everything was ready for school tomorrow.
But when she seemed to have disappeared for far too long the husband went looking. John found her sitting on their son's bed with their family photo in hand, reduced to silent tears yet again. How was Patrick not to see that something was wrong with his mother then?

When Patrick made it back he parked his bike back in the garage and entered the house through the back door. Immediately when he saw his mother in the living room with his father and in a better mood than she was when he left, he asked "Hey mom! What are we having for

lunch today?" He continued "I hope something sweet with a lot of sugar. I learnt sugar gives energy, and we all need energy, right?" They all laughed.
"But too much sugar will eat away your teeth!" the mother warned lightly and added a joke "But I think you'll look more handsome without teeth! So what do you want for lunch today, Pete?"
"Yes!" Patrick uttered coming to squeeze himself between his parents on the brown two sitter couch that was among a few others of the same design but different sizes in the open living room.
After thinking for a few seconds he said "I want pizza for lunch, is it okay, mom?" and quickly added, "With coke too. Oh and dad finished the last of the raisins, we should get another bag."
"Did he now!" the mother looked into the face of the father, "I guess your father needs energy too! You know what! Let's eat out today. In fact let's eat out every Sunday from now on." The mother suggested in reflection of the number of Sundays she had left on this earth...

Five weeks subsequent to her devastating diagnosis, the wife, the mother, got visibly ill from the virus. And Patrick seemed to worry more than his father, but it was simply because John Mot knew what was going on, and Patrick knew nothing of her mother's ailing condition. Alice Mot's sickness escalated from bad to worse as she got weaker by the passing of each day.
The mother in her probable last days tried her best to give advices in advance to her son, advices he would need later in his life, she thought and believed, but the son was not listening. Whenever John allowed Patrick into his mother's room, Patrick would sit there next to her bed and look at her with only one wish in his mind. He wished that he was all grown up and a 'doctor' by then, just so he could heal his mother. He even on some nights stayed out after dark on the lawn awaiting the dash of a shooting star above. Sadly he never caught sight of one, but made the wish regardless. He wished on every night to the stars above when awaiting the shooting star to become a medical doctor when he grew up, just so he could see her smile again, laugh again, and even shout at him when he does something she didn't agree with.

A few of her colleagues visited. And those who couldn't visit wished her a speedy recovery in cards embedded in bunches of flowers. The kids sent balloons and wrote some of the most beautiful words on bright colored cards, some even took the effort to leave drawings for her. To some of the patients at the hospital she was a second mother.

And one card out of all touched her heart the most that the mother in her probable last days smiled for the first time in weeks, and cried not of her pain, but joy. This young girl who had written a card did not write it to her, but to Patrick instead! In it comforting the boy and asking him to be strong, for her mother. And at the end of the card she wrote '*come to the hospital someday, I'd like to meet you Pete, I'll be your friend... from Seanokeng with care.*'
With all the strength she had left in her Alice raised that special card to Patrick who stood above her, with teary eyes still she looked up into his face and smiled "Look at you, you look just like him, you really are your father's son." She said in a frail voice "And like your father you are gonna marry a nurse one day, you're gonna love her, she already does you." and went on to add "You should go see her, she's not gonna be at the hospital forever." She handed him the card and those were her last words. Till her dying breath she would speak no more, and not out of choice, it was the virus, it had taken that ability to speak from her...

For Mrs. Mot zero hour approached - April second, the year 2012 - the rising sun rose with her demise as her time of death was pronounced at six thirty in the morning. Patrick understood nothing of it all - all he knew was that death had taken his mother away from him. Weirdly, he was not even sad about it - just perplexed about the whole thing.
While the son stood puzzled at what had happened to his mother, the father was drowning in a pool of his own tears as if he was unaware that the very last day was approaching, and very fast at it even. It could be argued that he had the time to prepare for it. But the truth is; no one really can prepare for the loss of those they hold dear to themselves...

The service of the funeral was held on Friday the sixth of April - a day celebrated as GOOD FRIDAY by Christians. The service was at the birth place of the late Alice M. Mot, and during the whole interval of the funeral Patrick didn't show any signs of emotional ache - no tear or even a sad face for him. His face was rather filled with curiosity, and misplaced wonders. All he ever thought about that day was how all that happened - how does death happen that is, and what was of his mother then, an invisible ghost? Hovering about within the crowd that had attended his mother's farewell service, he even thought that maybe if he concentrated and listened hard enough he might hear her '*wooing*' in the air...

Two days after the interment, on a Sunday, Patrick and his father journeyed back home.
The drive back home to Roseville was unspoken - the only sound that was made in that four hours thirty minutes drive was that of the humming engine of the big black Audi Q7.
Patrick had so much on his mind that he wanted to ask his father, but knowing that doing so will only evoke his father's subsided painful emotions, he kept his questions to himself, even his distant self could see how broken his father was...

The schools reopened on the tenth of April. Who was better suited for Patrick to ask his questions concerning death to other than his mentor, friend and Natural Sciences teacher? Mr. Alfred Maoto Tobetsa - 'Mr. T' as the kids called him, liked spending time with curious Patrick. He lived only a five minutes bicycle ride from Patrick's home, and it is there that Patrick spent most of his weekdays' afternoons, conducting experiments with his Sciences teacher in his house laboratory.

On the first day of the second term during break time Patrick went to the school lab where he spent all his break times with Mr. T. The two interacted more like brothers rather than like teacher and pupil.
"Hello! Mr. T! Are you in here?" Patrick called out entering the lab.
It was a two roomed building separated from all the other buildings in the primary school. One room was for the paper work where Patrick and Mr. T sat to eat and talk. The other room was the lab with all chemicals and all scientific tools for Science experiments.
The teacher in his thirties emerged from under a meter high table that had concealed his not so lean body perfectly, "Patrick!" He greeted the boy before him with a sigh of relief. "I thought you were the men in blue." Added the relieved teacher referring to the police as the 'men in blue' while pulling the chair he was sitting on before hiding under the table.
"Tax evasion again?" Patrick asked putting his foods on the table that was dead fastened to the floor and pulling a chair to sit down as well.

"Nah!" there was a smug on his face as he corrected in a bragging manner "Tax EVASIONS!"
"Mr. T, I know this afternoon at your house we're supposed to look into the LIFE BEYOND EARTH topic." The youngster began "But I think I have something bigger we should look into." while gazing at a human skeleton chart pasted on the near white painted wall of the room.

"OK." Mr. T affirmed and added not doubting the youngster claiming that what he had to talk to him about later on was 'big', merely because Patrick had countless times in the past presented the teacher with the most ingenious ideas he's ever heard, and the fact that they were coming from a young boy no older than fourteen even impressed him more, "As long as it's something that will not make me throw up this time, Patrick!" both laughed at the memory of that incident.
More than half an hour later the bell ending the lunch interval rang and Patrick had to rush back to class...

At approximately three in the afternoon Patrick had come back from school, his father had not yet returned from his work.
Four slices of buttered bread into his lunch box he got on his bike with his back pack on his back and rode to Mr. T's house.
When he got there, he made sure to chain his bike to a pole in Mr. T's yard just on the edge of the mowed lawn surrounded by colorful daisies. He had learnt his lesson the last time he left his bike exposed to theft - rude teens helped themselves to it, but something good came out of it for his father replaced it with his current blue BMX bike.
Patrick didn't bother to knock, he entered the bachelor's five roomed house and put his back pack on top of the black dinner table.
The interior of the house had the evident touch of a woman, a long dead white woman that is, a sad story Mr. T did reckless and stupid things to try to forget till Patrick came to his rescue.
"Patrick! Is that you?" Mr. T asked from the TV room, but before Patrick could reply, he was already entering the kitchen, "Did you bring it?" he asked rubbing his palms together in an anticipative crave.
"Have I ever left it?" Patrick answered with a question pointing at the back pack on top of the table.
Mr. T really loved Mrs. Mot's buttered bread - he always said that it was the best.
The thirty something year old bachelor also preferred to keep to himself not concerning himself with anything that did not affect him in any way, thus even though the death of the most decorated local children's hospital's nurse had been published in the local newspaper from the second day after her death up to then, which was then over a week since her passing, he knew absolutely nothing of it. And even though he and John were friends, the best of, John never bothered to call him and tell the sad news.

"Get the lab coats." said Mr. T while reaching for the back pack. He chewed on the bread and after the first swallow he started to shake his head in disagreement, "Patrick.. this tastes different." He complained.
"You'll know why...soon enough " Patrick replied throwing the other lab coat to Mr. T who seemed rather confused by the response.
The two entered an air tight room that was next to the TV room and opposite the kitchen. Mr. T closed the heavy titanium door behind them - this room was his home laboratory.
"How far are you with the frog research?" Patrick asked staring at a chart that showed the internal structure of a bull frog, pasted on the white idea board.
"Where you left me the last time you were here. We still have three we haven't dissected." He replied with a suggestion "So...while we talk about what you supposedly say is more interesting than LIFE BEYOND EARTH, I mean come on P! What could be better than aliens? We'll dissect one."
Patrick was already clearing the dissecting board, "What are you waiting for? Get the frogs." They both put on surgical gloves and masks.

"So what did you want to talk about?" Mr. T asked putting a fish tank with three bull frogs in it on top of the counter.
"I wanna talk about death." Patrick began off the top without warming him up for it "What is death? And how does it all happen?"
"Whoa! I didn't expect that." Mr. T was equally shocked as he was impressed with Patrick's interest on death at such an immature age that even raised little concern, "Well scientifically, death is when a living organism seizes to live, in simple tense...death is the end of life as we know it. Sooner or later we all die...all living things do." Mr. T continued to explain all there was to death to Patrick whom listened like his life depended on it, in his head it actually did.

After a few hours of talking about mortality while dissecting innocent bull frogs in the name of *Science* as the two would always excuse their brutality to the animals, Patrick turned to the clock that was hung on the wall "It's getting late, I should get going." He stated placing the silver blades into a dry sink and took off both the gloves and the mask and would also the lab coat just outside the room.
"You're right." Mr. T agreed "It's a school day tomorrow. We wouldn't want your dad coming here for you again, would we? I'll walk you out."

The two came out of the laboratory and walked towards the kitchen door which was also the front door, "Don't forget your back pack." said Mr. T.
"Oh! I almost forgot...the buttered bread tasted different because mom didn't butter it, I did...and she never will." Patrick informed with a neutral tone.
"Why is that? Am I finishing your butter?" Mr. T asked jokingly, and had he known why she would butter the bread no more he wouldn't have.
"Mom died a week ago." Patrick broke the news to him.
"Oh...I didn't know, lad..." He was shocked "I'm sorry, I really am."
"I'm not." Patrick quickly replied, "Everyone keeps saying they are, you know...But I think they are lying. They didn't even know my mom. How could they be sorry if they never knew her?" And the two got out the house with Mr. T asking young Patrick if that was the reason he wanted to know so much more about death and Patrick affirmed. But the teacher was secretly concerned of how the boy seemed to be dealing with the passing of his own mother.

By six thirty that evening Patrick was already back home, but was delayed outside tending to the little dirt on his bike.
His father had come back from work by then. He sat lonely in the dark without even noticing it, his teary eyes reflected back at him on the television screen.
"Hey dad..." Patrick greeted and immediately added "Mr. T says he's sorry about mom's death." And switched on the lights, but his father wouldn't let him see his tears. Without response John just stood up from where he sat and went to his room.
Patrick could hear him turning the locking mechanism on his bedroom door to lock it, a trait he just adopted after his wife's death. He was still in bereavement and didn't seem to be getting better emotionally with the passing of time, he was rather getting worse as it seemed.

Patrick warmed his foods that his father had cooked and placed in the oven for him. He went to his room to fetch his school bag. He always preferred to write his home-works whilst eating and watching cartoons at the same time. And whenever Mrs. Mot, his departed mother, would ask him to stop he would always answer by saying 'I'm multitasking mom' with a goofy smile.
That night Patrick could not stop thinking about what Mr. T had told him about death. He thought of that till he fell asleep in his room.

Morning came - Mr. Mot left an hour before Patrick woke, but he had prepared everything that Patrick would need for school just as his late mother would.
John was actually on the other hand relieved that his son wasn't affected by the passing of his mother that much, though at times he feared that Patrick might be bottling up his emotions. And would let it all out some of these days, and he preferred that it would be sooner rather than later in his life as the ripples of the emotional explosion would be much smaller at his adolescent age than it would be when he's much older...

End of year school closing day arrived - December seventh, the year 2012 - a day when pupils got their report cards that showed how each and every pupil had worked individually that year, and also determining if that individual pupil should proceed to the next grade or not. Patrick's report card showcased that he had really worked hard that year, but the truth was that he did not at all. All he just did was try his best to remember what was said to him by the teachers whenever required to do so, and added in as well an unhealthy amount of general knowledge, something he was well known for by all his teachers. But they learnt to refrain from praising and naming or calling him the genius of his class, for some reason he always frowned at anyone would dare call him a genius or praised him for his high IQ...

"I made it man...I'm going to eighth grade." His voice joyous and a smile on his face said it all, that he was happy as he entered through the open door, and subsequently broke into a song and dance. He sang, horribly, and wiggled worse than he sang. He just wasn't a good dancer. Dance was what he'd do if he wanted to give his parents a good laugh.
"That's great lad! But you know who will be happier to hear that? Your dad." said Mr. T to Patrick with a smile expressing pride over the boy.
"Yeah, that's why I came here...to let you know that I will not be coming around today, I know for sure that my dad will take me out to celebrate this achievement." Mr. Mot had not gone to work that morning and he hadn't been going for a week. Patrick figured he was on end of year leave or something, "Plus I haven't seen him smile in a while." He added gazing at his own sneakers as if analyzing them for faults - it was the last day of school of that year which allowed pupils not to be in their school uniforms if they desired so and Patrick wasn't in his.
"Why are you still here then? Don't keep an old man waiting, and

hey...don't tell him I called him old, okay?" Mr. T pleaded with Patrick whom had already turned to the doorway. And needed not to see the lad's report card for himself, he knew exactly what was on it; an overall mark of over seventy five percent in all nine subjects with both languages, the first additional and the home language with high scores of eighty three and eighty seven percents respectively.
The three - but two then - most influential people in his life knew he could score more in other subjects as well, but the lad was not so keen on doing that. One thing he hated was to stand out. He hated it when he was the only one who knew answers to certain questions, hated it more when he had to answer them out loud.
Thirty seconds later, Patrick rushed back into the school laboratory and almost took a nasty spill all the while giving a fright to Alfred who was already buried in a book, "Almost forgot!" he said as he headed straight for the whiteboard.
"What is it, P?" he asked first and warned after "One of these days you gonna break a leg."
"Yeah I know, but you know me, I'll walk it off." He returned smugly and grabbed a non-permanent marker, "Since this is my last day in a here I thought I should leave something behind!" he said and wrote on the board with his crooked hand writing, 'Patrick N. Mot was here.' He turned to the door.
"But you know that can be erased by anyone, anytime with no trouble at all, right?" Said Alfred amused by what the boy had turned back to do, "That's no permanent marker, kid!" He informed.
Patrick turned to him, "I know." He said and quickly added, "But by that time someone erases it the phrase would have taken proper hold in your memory. I could care less if anyone else sees it, but I want you to remember it, always."
Before Alfred could reply to the boy's remarkable gesture Patrick jetted out screaming "See you tomorrow at four, old man!"

He stopped nowhere else, headed straight for home. He couldn't wait to get there - his jog augmented into a sprint that he maintained for a while. He was most likely the fastest kid of his age in his school, but never had interests in joining the school junior athletics team.
He stopped at the front gate to his home. It wasn't that he was too tired. He stopped to look at a board suspended on a pole next to the gate. It grabbed his attention since it wasn't there in the morning when he left for school. And it was in red.

The board had a phrase that read 'FOR SALE' with a red line running through it, and underneath that 'FOR SALE' phrase on the same board another phrase read 'SOLD' with bolder letters even.
He slid open a small gap on the gate, enough for him to walk through and walked towards the house. He tried at the front door but it did not open, he had to unlock it first and it could only mean his father wasn't home. He unlocked it with the copy of the front door key he carried with him.
When he entered the house, he could not believe his eyes. The house was so empty that he heard the echoes of his voice as he called out for his father. He called several times standing puzzled only a few paces from the front door in the inside of the hollow house, but no one answered back. His eyes searched for anything that might give him an idea of what was going on other than the sign at the gate, which suggested something crazy in his head. Crazy, but with the state the house was in, it was most likely true. As the old saying goes; whenever you eliminate the impossible, whatever remains, no matter how improbable, is the truth.
The house looked as if no one had ever lived in it, everything was gone. Even his mother's favorite portraits of early civilization that hanged orderly on the wall had been removed, leaving the wall as clear as the winter skies. The only things that remained were the curtains on the windows.
Giving up on solving the mystery of the empty house he walked to his bedroom, but it too was as empty as the rest of the house. Except that right in the middle of it there laid a brown wooden box that seemed to have been purposely placed by someone who really wanted it to be seen or found.
The lid of the box read "IDENTITY" with an italic font. After picking it up he moved in reverse towards the wall of the side where his study table used to be. He sat down with his back against the wall and opened the box. Inside of it was a black normal-sized journal and underneath it his birth certificate. Only the first six pages of the journal had writings on them, he quickly recognized the hand writing to be that of his father, he read the entries…

The journal read *"I leave this as a declaration of intent, so you will not be confused:*
One; son, things aren't sequential as I might have thought. Good doesn't always lead to good, nor does bad always lead to bad.

Two; Those who choose to love stand a better chance of finding happiness in this brief existence, but run the risk of losing that which they love and hold dear to themselves. But those who choose not to love run the greater risk of having to carry the burden of solitude and the hatred from others. But spare themselves the pain of loss.
Three; I will hate and not be able to live with myself if you were to go through the same suffering as I did as a boy and do now after losing your mother. My disappearance is to refuse you the pain of losing loved ones. You will hate me now, that's good. Use that rage to break through whatever may be in conflict with your ideas of what you want to do in this cursed world..." The journal went on to explain the motives of Mr. Mot's sudden disappearance. But nothing, even grief, could or should justify his actions. Parental responsibilities are one of the few you never get to relinquish, period, regardless of circumstance.

Patrick after reading the intentions of his dad, stood up from where he sat and walked out of his hollow room. Out the back door he walked to the garage, but in it too there wasn't evidence of anything ever being in it - his bike and the two cars were not there. Out the garage he walked straight to the gate.
Regardless how real it was, along his slow walk to a familiar place where he'd seek sanctuary, he kept thinking that he'd wake up on his bed in his bedroom and realize how all that was just a dream. A dream he'd surely convey to his father when he wakes! But sadly it was not a dream, his father was gone and without a trace.

He knocked, but like always, he never waited for the permission to enter the house. He walked straight to the television room and found Mr. T watching a movie and eating something while at the same time going through some paperwork from school - those two had a lot in common than they cared to admit or even realize.
"Hey man, can I join you?" Patrick made the request walking behind the couch Alfred was seated on - he had just arrived from school.
Mr. T turned and asked "Shouldn't you be with your dad celebrating or something? Where is he?" he lazily peaked behind Patrick.
"He wasn't home." he said evenly and tossed the wooden box over to Alfred, "And by the looks of it he ain't coming back."
After reading the journal himself he held it up back to him, "You do know that normal people do this on a day called 'April's fool', right?" Alfred was as amused as he was impressed, "It's a good one though." he praised.

"Can you please call him." said Patrick, "Maybe you're right. Maybe this is all a practical joke, on both of us. Because I'm not in on it" He added. Even though he knew the un-likeliness of it being as Alfred ruled it, he hoped. But the calls to Patrick's father would not go through; they all went straight to voice mail prompts.
A couple of minutes later Patrick had convinced his mentor to drive by his home with him so he could see for himself. He refused to believe that John had really done 'it'.
But after he saw the house, he would not doubt it, Patrick's father was gone, and without a trace.
Alfred thought what John Mot had done to his son was wrong. He had talked with John about it, and even he had seen its reasons, or rather necessity, he never thought John would go through with it. But he would not share it with Patrick. And part of him looked forward to having Patrick stay with him till relatives who lived far outside of Roseville were informed and a legal decision of guardianship was made. And that would give him something like a month with the boy.
"What now?" Patrick asked.
But before Mr. T could say anything back, there sounded a loud bang at the front door. When he asked who it was behind the door, a deep firm voice accompanied the bangs, "This is the police, open up the door!"

"To what do I owe the presence of the men in blue?" Mr. T thought to himself as he walked from the TV room to the front door, "It might be about your dad, lad." he briefly turned to Patrick, concealing the concern that came with the idea that the police might be there about Patrick's father. Maybe he had done something that left him with only one choice, flee.
Immediately after he opened the door a giant of a black policeman asked "Sir! Is your name Alfred Maoto Tobetsa?" accompanied by a white emaciated officer who kept his eyes on Patrick whom approached the scene slowly, doubting if the policemen would allow him to be there when they conduct their business with his mentor, or whatever it was that brought them there.
"So it said on my ID card the last time I checked." Mr. T answered back with little surprise to the police unannounced visit to his house, for he quickly suspected the other reason the police might be there.
The big policeman looked Mr. T dead in the eyes and spoke firmly while reaching for the handcuffs hanging on the waist belt he wore as part of the national police uniform, "Sir, I hereby place you under

arrest for the numerous criminal offences of tax evasions. You have the right to remain silent. Anything you say may and will be used against you in the court of law. You have the right to an attorney of your choice. If you cannot afford one, the state will provide one for you, free of charge. Should you choose to comply and come with us nicely, I will not have to use these in front of your son." He raised the handcuffs to Alfred.
"You are like twice my size. I have no choice but to comply." The teacher replied with a bit of humor in his tone, "But can I please have a word with my son, please, I promise to come nicely after." he requested. Hoping to sway the big man's response in his favor he wiped the grin from his face, and for the first time since learning that missing your taxes was actually a crime his face actually showed the seriousness of the matter.
"You've got five minutes...we'll be waiting at the car, and don't try anything funny." said the thin white Policeman. "Five minutes and nothing funny!" he repeated in warning, and both policemen turned to walk back to their car.

"Did you hear that? He called you my son." Mr. T began at Patrick after pushing close the front door.
"I did warn you...so what now?" Patrick asked, and deeply hoped that the circumstance would not affect Alfred's decision to let him stay with him for the time being since he had nowhere else to go. They hand not placed the call to his relatives yet.
"Don't worry man, you still get to stay here. Better yet...you get to be the man of the house." Said Mr. T, and paused to say "I'll probably be sentenced to two years and be out in a few months due to good behavior. Hopefully you'll still be here."
"You sound like you've been to prison before, have you?" Patrick asked.
"Nah..." he replied, "In my bedroom, which will now be your bedroom, there's a safe. The combination is the molar mass and atomic number of an oxygen atom respectively, use whatever is in the safe on whatever you wish and the pin codes to the bank cards are similar to the safe's combination. This is not goodbye...this is see you in a few months. Oh!...And I recommend that you befriend the girl who lives opposite here, she's nice I tell you, and pretty! Your age too!"
"I'll be fine on my own, why make friends if I might not get to stay here that long, I think you should go before the big man comes in here to

drag you out." Patrick warned smiling in a situation they both should have been devastated in.

Both Patrick and Mr. T said their goodbyes to each other. When Alfred walked out the door, Patrick followed. The police car was just in front of the gate with both policemen standing against it.
Patrick watched standing halfway between the front door and the gate as Mr. T approached the police car.
Before entering the vehicle, he turned back at Patrick and waved with a smile. The two policemen entered the car and drove away with Mr. T in the back seat. They didn't have to use the cuffs as he complied just as he promised he would should they let him have a word with his 'son', and they did.
Patrick got back into the house, closed the door and stood before the lab door. His eyes fixed searchingly at the ceiling above he asked "What now?"

CHAPTER TWO: High school debut

A week following the mentor's apprehension - on a rather hot Sunday morning - Patrick would no longer sit around hoping for his father's return. He knew that it was only prudent to have means of communication with someone you've just bought a house from. He thought that if he went by his 'former' home, the new occupants might give him some information that might hint his father's whereabouts. By midday he was already on his way to his old home. And had to hope that the new occupants were not church people, for if they were, he would not find them home for it was a Sunday.
The gate was not locked, someone had to be home, he figured. Everything looked the same as it did when he still lived there, not that so much could've change in a week regardless the home having new owners.
The flowering garden was a spectacle to gaze upon still. The red and the white roses were high growing and the bright daisies did not fall short behind. The grass on the lawn had just been trimmed and was looking greener than ever, the sprinklers had just been turned off no more than an hour ago it seemed looking at the damp dirt around the lawn.
Patrick turned his eyes to the small garden of home grown veggies, and remembered how he had convinced his father to agree to help him pick those that were ripe over the first weekend of his end of year school holidays. The two, Patrick and his father, would deliver them to the local children's hospital kitchen, just as his mother used to. And he hoped when there he'd for the first time finally meet the mysterious 'Seanokeng'. Yet felt like he already knew the girl, for his mother would always speak so often and highly of her. What Patrick did not know was that his mother had done the same of him to the girl, spoke so often and highly of her own son to her. So often that the girl had the highest sense of who Patrick was, best qualities and worst, she knew them all from the boy's mother herself. So when Alice would see the girl she meant to adopt slowly but surely fall in love with a boy she was yet to meet it did not surprise her. It could be agreed that it's every mother's role to play match maker once or twice in the lives of their daughters and sons. Sadly this one mother had passed away not knowing if she had failed or succeeded.

Patrick stood before the front door, but he would not knock. A minute's length standing there like a robot he just turned and walked away without questioning his decision. Right then he decided that he would not look for his father. If his father wanted him he would've not sold the house and disappeared, he would have stayed with him or at the least took him along to wherever he disappeared to, but he did not. His own father did not want him, Patrick convinced himself, and right then the hate for his own father was born...

Two weeks since the arrest. Mr. T's trial was set to be on a Wednesday of that week.
In that short interval Patrick had adapted to the life of solitude. He used the money that Alfred told him was in the safe as well as the credit cards and debit cards to kick-start his life without either of his parents. He bought all he needed as well as some things he wanted, mostly for entertainment; a few electronics were ought to do it. But a cell phone he never bought, and he's only defense against getting one was; 'who would I call?'
Wednesday - trial day - he woke up at exactly six o'clock in the morning, made himself breakfast, took a bath and prepared to go to the court that Mr. T was going to be trialed at. It was located in the nearest town from Roseville.

By ten thirty that morning Patrick was in the courtroom. He sat at the front row next to two teachers who were colleagues of Mr. T's. There was no one who was there as a relative to Mr. T - did they choose not to come? Or did he even have any? That was a question only Alfred could answer, or maybe they didn't know of the trial. Come to mention it, the only people who were in the courtroom in support of Mr. T were only the two teachers and Patrick. The rest of the attendants were people who had come early for cases that were to follow after Mr. T's.

The defendant, Alfred, appeared from what seemed like a basement room with two guards by his sides who led him to where he was supposed to stand. The judge entered the courtroom and after he sat down the court proceedings began.
Alfred was already found guilty for the multiple crimes. The court proceedings were simply for his lawyer - provided by the state without any fees - to try and get a lower sentence for Alfred, and his chances of getting that were great as he was a first time offender, but the judge would shock everyone in the room with his final verdict.

In the final moments of the thirty minutes of the case deliberation the judge ordered silence and began, "Mr. Alfred Maoto Tobetsa, in the multiple charges of tax evasions, you're found guilty, this trial will serve as a warning to those who deliberately miss paying their taxes knowing that when they are caught they will be sentenced to light sentences, that ends today." The judge continued with his voice uplifted by annoyance and disgust "Mr. Tobetsa, you're sentenced to ten years in prison with no chance of a reduced sentence for crippling the economy of this country. Guards! Take him away." He ordered with his eyes burning at Alfred whom stood unshaken by the judge's decision.

Two guards came to Mr. T's sides - the very two that brought him into the courtroom.
But before being 'escorted' away by the two guards in dark-brown uniforms, Alfred had one plea to make to the judge. He referred to Patrick as his son and asked the judge to allow him to have a few last words with him. The judge allowed it, he too bought the 'father and son' story just as everyone else in the courtroom did, and simply because there was no reason to believe or suspect otherwise. Only the two teachers in the front row knew of the deception; and it was because over the years in their primary school they had once or twice taught their respective subjects to Patrick and have met his real father and mother over teacher and parent meetings.
Mr. T called out to Patrick by the wave of his chained hand.

Patrick seemed unaffected by the judge's harsh sentence as well, but that wasn't surprising as that was the very same kid who didn't even shed a single tear at the passing of his own mother or panicked when he found out that his father had ran out on him and left him with nothing.
He approached and stood in front of Mr. T who was standing between the two guards still.
Alfred rested his heavy hand but with a gentle touch on Patrick's shoulder and began "Hey man...seems like I'm going in for a longer time than I had anticipated, but this should give you enough time to complete it." He paused to say "I would really like to see it work, let alone let you try it on me."
"What are you talking about?" Patrick asked with a good idea of what Mr. T was talking about, he just wanted to confirm his suspicion.

Alfred leaned down to Patrick and whispered in his ear "Immortality." Patrick asked again "You know about that?"
He stood back upright "Of course, I know everything that goes on in my house." He replied "I've known for a while now, but I did not want to get involved, I realized that you work best on your own, son, good luck with it."
Since his mother's death over the months to his father's disappearance Patrick had been working in Mr. T's lab with a different motive than when he first entered the lab years ago. He was researching topics that he explained to Mr. T as simply appealing to research, but Mr. T knew of the real reason for the researches and often gave the lad space to work.
"I don't need luck." Said Patrick with cockiness expressed on his face.
"I know you don't...see you in a decade lad." Mr. T replied, then the guards took him away and people started to prepare for the next case.
Patrick left the courtroom following behind the two teachers who were in discussion of how harsh the judge's ruling was based on the crime their colleague committed.

The first weekend after the trial - on a Saturday - Patrick woke with the intent to spend the whole day in the house laboratory with an aim to crack and exploit the secrets and facts that comes with mortality, 'loop holes' he called them.
He entered the lab at approximately eight thirty in the morning - right after his filling breakfast.
Inside the lab he stared at the idea board and said to himself "This will be a long day."
He did not vacillate to start writing his ideas on the board while he talked to himself. From time to time the fourteen year old tended to do that, talking to himself that is, and referred to it as rather talking 'with' himself than talking 'to' himself.

The youngster wrote on the board while in deep conversation with himself till he finally accepted two theories to work on with hopes of curing his own mortality; 'first theory' and 'second theory' so he named them, and summarized them on the idea board.
"FIRST THEORY; CROSS GENETICS to achieve a state of ACCELERATED CELLULAR REGENERATION...
SECOND THEORY; BRAIN TRANSPLANTATION into a healthier SUBSTITUTE BODY...
Perfecting one of these procedures will guarantee immortality..." He

captioned.
After ten minutes of writing on the board Patrick paced a meter backwards, stared proudly at what he had scribbled on the board and said "Damn, I'm good!" He continued the scribbling.
The work he's been doing since the death of his mother in Mr. T's lab seemed to be finally paying off.
He exited the house lab exhausted a few hours past noon; it seemed he had accomplished what he had intended to do when he woke that morning - spending the whole day in his mentor's lab.

After a long day in the laboratory working on a farfetched idea, there was nothing in the kitchen the youngster felt like eating to satisfy his hunger, he had to head to the closest mini market for something sugary most probably.
As soon as he walked out the house there 'she' was, pretty as a perfect summer day, his future wife, struggling to open her home's gate - the girl who lived opposite Alfred's house. It was the same girl whom Mr. T had advised Patrick on the day of his arrest that it would be nice to befriend. Even distant Patrick admitted it to himself that she was pretty, and she seemed his age if not a little younger than him.
The girl and her little sister had come to live with their aunt just two weeks before the final school closing day for that year. She was in the same grade as Patrick, but had attended a different primary school; it was on the far-East side of Roseville close to where she lived with her other aunt whom had to relocate for employment reasons.
The two siblings had been bouncing from one aunt to the next since the tragic passing of their mother. A father no matter how responsible he might be, he's always argued in black traditions to be the right person to raise a young lady, let alone two.

"There's no turning back now." Thought Patrick as he walked closer to Mr. T's gate and would soon be walking past her if she couldn't get her gate opened by then.
He initiated a plan, to keep walking without turning her way no matter what. But could not stay loyal to that plan as he stopped and listened immediately when she called out to him, "Hey, can you help me out here, please!" she politely asked.
It was the first time Patrick was hearing her voice and would be the first time she was going to hear Patrick's if he was to reply to her. But he did not reply. He just stood there in the middle of the street frozen with his nerves flaring in all directions. Patrick had never in his life

spoken socially to a girl his age before. Except at school, and would be terrified throughout the conversation minding his every word.
"This old rusted thing does not want to open up." her voice was sweet and inviting even when she complained, "I've been at it for over two minutes now, and it still won't push open." her face clearly showed the frustration, yet it somehow made the features of her bright face to come out only to intensify her beauty rather than mask it.

He fiddled with his digital wrist watch first before making that terrifying ninety degree turn to face her. Slowly he approached. Without making direct or any eye contact with her he began just after briefly observing the gate "It is old and rusted...but I don't think that's the reason it's not opening." He pushed the gate in the closing direction and pulled out a pebble that had been stuck on the track of the gate. "I think you should try it again." He said.
Mesmerized and lost in hearing the vibrating sound of his pubescent thickening voice she delayed her response.
Shockingly the gate slid open with ease when she tried at it. When she turned to make eye contact he resisted, but she began anyway "Wow! Thanks a lot! You live here right? What's your name?"
"My name is Patrick, Patrick Mot, and yes, I do live here." Said Patrick as he still refused her a glimpse into his eyes and turned to walk away. Had he looked up he'd have seen how her face lit up as he paused and repeated his first name adding in his last. She had never heard a teenage boy introduce himself like that before. Like a man of profound status, a gentleman! Right then at that moment from how he figured the problem with her gate and 'fixed' it, to how he spoke, all the way to how he rigidly held his posture yet refusing her even one gaze into his eyes, she knew. She knew that she liked him, or at the least would.

"Hey wait! Aren't you going to ask me my name?" She asked trying to make the conversation lengthier. Without a reply he stopped, but did not turn to her.
"My name is Hannah, and I live here, obviously!" a friendly smile curved on her lips, but was pointless as it went unnoticed by the boy before her.
"I know." Patrick replied and turned to her, he still fiddled with his wrist watch. An adopted calming mechanism and it worked, so he believed.
"And how do you know that, Patrick Mot?" she inquired enunciating his names.

For the first time he raised his eyes to bravely meet hers, "You just told me, remember?" He replied complementing the girl's smile with his own that disappeared as soon as it came.
Her smile gave way to a silent laugh, exposing her front teeth. For a moment their eyes were interlocked. Patrick was caught up into staring into her eyes as much as she was into his. The color allotments of her eyes were unusual, but it was their oddness that made them that attractive to the eye, that even Patrick couldn't resist taking a long peek into them.
Had they stared into each other's eyes in that silence any longer than they already had, it was only going to get more awkward between the two, so, to end the eye contest Patrick asked "Can I go now?" without waiting for her to answer he turned and walked away with his left hand dipped into his pocket.
"Wow! She's even more beautiful up close!" He thought to himself as he walked further away. And something about her behavior felt rather familiar like he had interacted with her before, but he had not.
"*Patrick Mot!*" She said silently to herself, and for a moment at that gate she had totally forgotten if she was coming in or going out. And the harder she tried to listen to her thoughts, the clearer it was to hear the echoes of Patrick's masculine voice as he introduced himself. She had just met him, but was missing him already. She wondered how long it would be before she would talk to him again, yet dreaded the likely answer to that. The boy rarely got out of the house.
In Hannah too it existed, that feeling of familiarity like she had known him before yet the two were only meeting for the very first time. So how was it that they both felt like they had talked or seen each other before? Maybe that's how mutual attraction works, you both feel like you've seen the other person before, maybe that's all it was...

That time of the year - the festive season - kids his age eagerly waited for Christmas day; to open the presents that they'll be receiving from those who cared for them. Patrick too used to look forward to Christmas day every year. Actually, that year's Christmas was going to be the first he would spend alone without his parents, a first of many to come without both of his parents or either parent since his father ran out and left no scent of intentions of getting back to his son.

Days passed and the inevitable came - Patrick's first Christmas day without his parents or anyone for that matter.
It was already after midday and he was still feeling normal as usual, his

kind of 'normal' anyway. But reality got to him when he switched ON the television and saw that even his regular afternoon programs were disturbed by Christmas day special programs.
He tried numerous stations trying to find something to watch other than reminders of what he had lost that year, a mother, a father and in a way, a mentor. In thoughts "*This must be the longest day of this year, they say everyone is happy on Christmas, I'm not, I guess I'm not part of 'everyone', this will do.*" Patrick settled for an animal show on National Geography Wild. His legs stretched he laid back comfortably on the couch.
And out of nowhere a knock at the door! Knocks were very rare in that house, even when Alfred was still around.
Patrick went to open the door. And there he was, in the flesh, his own father, standing at the doorway before him. "Dad...?" Patrick uttered softly staring at his father with great awe, he couldn't believe it.
Mr. Mot realizing that his son had frozen in shock broke the ice "Aren't you going to let me in, son?"
Patrick quickly made way for his father to walk through. He silently led him to the TV room from behind.
"Look what I brought." Said the father revealing the contents of a plastic bag he carried with him. "Say we make up for lost time, what you say?" John inquired.
"No way!" he couldn't believe his eyes yet again, "These video games just hit the market, and how did you get them?" He asked overwhelmed by what his dad had brought him for Christmas. At that moment Patrick didn't seem to care that the very same man who stood before him ran out on him to fend for himself. All that mattered to him was that his father was back.
The two played video games like old times, victory or defeat, their voices would not lower. For the first time in weeks, Patrick was smiling and laughing, he was happy again.
Hours passed, and natural light began to dim. John Mot stood slowly to switch on the lights.
His eyes heavy, Patrick stretched his arms and yawned loudly with a wide open mouth. But his father would not sit back down. He stood above Patrick and looked down at him with a pitiful stare. "It's getting late." He said, "I'm sorry but you have to wake up, son."
All of the sudden it was dark in the house, like his father had just switched back OFF the lights. The light from the TV forcefully pierced into his eyes. Pinching them he looked away and slowly they began to

adjust to the darkness. But he could not see his father in the room, John was gone, so were the video games. It was all just a dream - Patrick had fallen asleep on the couch.
He stood from where he sat to switch ON the lights in the room "Seems I was wrong," He said "It's dark already. This was actually the shortest day of this year. Now what's to eat?" to himself and disappeared into the kitchen.

The fourteenth of January 2013 - a long anticipated Monday morning for the young Mot, it finally came to pass.
Patrick woke up with an anxious mind of the following day to come. He could not stop wondering about how his first day in his new school was going to be like. But most of all; he couldn't wait to put on his brand new uniform as well as the brand new back pack and see how he looked.
Around midday that Monday, after having a big meal of spaghetti with tomato sauce he took a rather quick bath and put on his brand new uniform to see if it fitted. After putting his back pack on he stood in front of the mirror his height in the bedroom and said "Not bad, not bad at all".
A smile that his face had long craved re-curved. For a moment the lonely teenager was cheered. But thinking about the reasons he smiled like that no more wiped the smile off his face and he slowly turned away from the mirror. He would spend the rest of the day with his brows drawn close together giving him that beetle-browed look.
He put the uniform on hangers and hanged it back inside the wardrobe where it had been hanging since he bought it a week after being accepted as a freshman in the local high school - Roseville High - not that far from Mr. T's house where Patrick lived then. He could've applied to the mixed race secondary school just outside Roseville, but having to use a bus everyday with dozens of other kids made him think otherwise about applying to be enrolled there...

Early hours of the morning, Patrick woke to prepare for his first day of school, better at it, first day of high school.
Still in the nude after the bath he paced to his room and pulled out his uniform to put it on. He stood in front of the mirror to see if everything was in line, then he remembered that he hadn't brushed his teeth.
The water he bathed in was still in the tub! The anxiety to his first day of high school was getting under his skin, in a way.
After brushing his teeth he made sure to flush the water in the bath tub

and even wiped clean and dry the inside of it. Cleaning up after himself was one of the great childhood habits that his mother bestowed upon him, or rather enforced onto him, not that any less could've been expected from Roseville's most decorated nurse towards her own and only child. And a son at it, a sex that is known to be most vulnerable to germs as they are 'handier' than their opposite sex...

He really looked good in his new uniform. Trousers pressed, long sleeved shirt straightened and tucked in, a black belt buckled, new black school shoes polished.
The only thing that was left to complete the uniform was the school tie. He had one. He had bought it along with the brand new uniform. And if he could tie it himself; he would've worn it, but regardless he looked sharp for his first day of school without it still. If only his parents could see him then, so he yeaned. A bigger boy, a bit grown up by then. And soon would need that fatherly guide through his rather late adolescence.
Outside the house - he closed the brown door and locked it. He turned to approach the gate minding every step with the shoes that he was stepping or rather walking outside in for the first time. He wouldn't want to get too much dust on them; thought would ruin the 'freshman look'.
With the gate he did the same as with the door; opened it and once on the other side closed it, locked it and turned to follow the road down to his new school. And right then, there she was; also departing for school.
From inside her home yard she called out to Patrick "Hey! Wait for me, would you?" her voice was friendly, no surprise there "You going to Roseville High?" she asked, secretly hoping that he could not tell of how she's been looking forward to talking to him again.

Patrick stopped and turned without saying a word, only nodded a 'yes' and thought "T*his is not good, this will be a long way to school, what do I even talk to her about along the way anyway?"* he raised his eyes to her and realized that she was struggling with the gate yet again. But that time around it was not pushing it open that she struggled with but rather unlocking the locking device on the gate, maybe it was old after all, just as old as she had mocked the other day.
Patrick approached and without greeting he began at her with his voice kept at neutral vibrations, not giving any signals to how he could've been feeling that morning, "Let me try it from this side." He

said.
Hannah without a pause gave him the keys and after his few attempts the lock unlocked. She rushed back to the house to return the keys and came back still rushing to get through the gate. "Let's go." she said and couldn't hide the fact that she was overjoyed for her first day of a new school year. And Patrick couldn't help but notice how close to him she walked. It made him so uncomfortable that he missed his walk rhythm one too many times, and his racing heart made matters worse. Yet he discreetly admitted that she looked prettier than she did the last time he was that close to her.
The silence he dreaded she so too hated that she had to ask "So…are you a freshman too?"
Patrick answered back without hesitation at all as if he had been waiting silently for her to ask that exact question "Yes." He dipped that left hand into his pocket and added "I bet you figured that by the brand new everything I'm wearing, right?"
"Kind of…" She answered back with her eyes scanning the lad's uniform and was she not going to sound really impressed she would've told him how she thought he looked in his uniform, sharp and 'gentleman-like' especially when he walked with one hand in his pocket like that. "Well…me too, I'm a freshman myself." She raised an eyebrow and added "or should I say…fresh-girl…"
Girls really have the ability to hide it when they are impressed and attracted in any way to the opposite sex. Hannah was impressed by Patrick's dressing and has been intrigued by his very drawn back life style from a social life ever since the youngster came to live right across from her new home. In the time she has come to live with her aunt she had never seen any boy over at Mr. T's or anyone for that matter. Though most would've picked up Patrick to be a weirdo, she thought of him very different and wanted to know more about the solitary teen.
"Or fresh-woman…" Said Patrick, but it came out wrong, and he quickly changed the 'freshman' topic, "So how long have you lived across from my place?" He asked and quickly added "because I've never seen you before till a few days before that day you asked me to help you with the gate."
"Wow!" she said blushingly, "You still remember, the first time we spoke." She has since that day anxiously been anticipating the next time she'll get to talk to him while on the other hand he dreaded it.
The conversation escalated as they talked about their separate primary

schools and what they'll miss about them; it was Hannah doing most of the talking of course. Patrick listened mostly and at some points she had to remind him that he had to keep saying 'yeses' and 'okays' to show that he really was listening.
At the end of their stroll; their destination premises - the Roseville high school, Roseville High or Rose-High as most called it, was the only high school within the Roseville walls.

The school was built very large just so to accommodate a large number of kids. Hannah had stopped talking at first sight of the school. Roseville high had at the least forty classes divided amongst five grades and a few other buildings like; the school kids toilets the size of two classes for each gender group, the teacher's open lounge, the Sciences' laboratory exactly the size of one class and a half divided into two rooms, the administrative area - where all managerial offices were situated - including the principal's office which all student which weren't freshmen in Roseville High feared being called to, since it was rarely ever for a good reason. The principal was well known for his old school disciplinary methods when it came to troublesome pupils.

It being their first time in the school they both didn't know where to head to after entering through the high gates. Patrick was he by himself would've wondered aimlessly till he found his way. But the girl he was with was not ashamed to ask for assistance.
Spotting someone who seemed to know his way "Hey!" she called out first, "Do you know where eighth graders are supposed to go?" she asked politely.
The tall light-brown skinned handsome boy was happy to help with the directions and was already eyeing Hannah, but what boy wouldn't, she was a beautiful girl. "You just have to go down this pavement and the last raw of classes down there on your left is where you want to be." He directed.
Hannah thanked, and she and Patrick followed the pavement as directed by the boy who would be her boyfriend in the year that would follow the next to come, but the boy's name then, Hannah didn't even know.

When they got to the eighth graders section Hannah saw a group of familiar faces, and she knew they were at the right place. She hadn't seen her friends since the last day of school December last year. They had a lot to catch up on.

The bright skinned girl with a single braided ponytail to hold back her long hairs turned to Patrick, "There! I found my friends and you better find yours too unless you wanna hang out with me and my loud friends." She said, "Who knows, maybe we'll get to share a class."
"I don't have friends." He answered in a low voice and never intended to be audible enough for her to hear him, but she did "And I doubt we'll be in the same class." He said turning away from her now with both hands dipped in his pockets and eyes low as if analyzing the grounds he walked upon. And the one thing that stuck with Hannah was how he said he doesn't have friends. In a way his tone suggested that he was actually okay with not having friends, that he actually preferred it and wasn't keen on making any anytime soon. So who would she be to him if he was not looking to make friends, she wondered...

"Just perfect." He thought as he got nearer to an isolated tree. Leaned against its trunk and from his back pack he pulled out a pen and a small pocket diary and started jotting some stuff down. But it was not a normal diary where one records his emotions and events of the day. His use for it was more complex than that.

When the eighth graders' teachers fanned out a group of senior boys to call all freshmen to come stand in front of the eighth grade section Patrick slowly but impatiently followed behind the mass of learners in brand new uniforms no different to his. They were going to be allocated classes.
He stood at the rear end of one of the lines. And when he caught sight of her, the girl who lived opposite him, get called forth and sent to the third class, he thought "C*hances that I get sent to that class? Let's see...about...pretty low*!" With a slight grin of relief on his face that no one could make out even if they looked his way.
Hannah's name was called before Patrick's on the list simply because she applied way before him and was enrolled first, thus her admission number came before Patrick's on the list.
His mind was so wrapped up around the concept of 'not that class' that he did not hear the teacher call out his name. The teacher had to call out a 'Patrick Mot' again and again with the pitch of voice intensifying in every call out. And eventually he heard her, by then the teacher was shouting out Patrick's name with a bit of anger in her voice, probably already thinking of moving on to the next name that followed after Patrick's on the list of countless freshmen to be given classes.
The fourteen year old raised his hand from behind the short cues so

that the teacher would notice him and would stop shouting his name. He pushed through the crowd still with the thought 'not that class' running laps in his head.

His fellow freshmen stared at him as he made his way up the two steps elevation to stand in front of the teacher, several if not more or less faces from primary school recognized him, they were his seventh grade classmates.

The teacher looked back at Patrick and it was evident on her face that she disliked what the young boy had just made her do; screaming his name out one too many times like that, "Patrick Mot, THIRD CLASS!" The teacher spoke with an intensified voice still. And the two words to Patrick felt like a punch to the chest, his heart started pounding as the words echoed in his ears. He thought his mind was playing tricks on him for he played the phrase 'not that class' in his head repeatedly. Pointing at the third class he asked for confirmation "That class?" His voice low and soft, humbler so as if pleading with the teacher not to be sent to 'that class' and for one known reason only; the girl who lived across from him, the same girl he walked to school with that day - was in that class. Why he wanted to avoid sharing a class with her? Only he knew.

The teacher confirmed, pointing at the same class as the boy before her was, "Yes, Mot, that class!" And Patrick could hear in her voice that she was still annoyed by the fact that she had to scream out his name too many times before he made his presence known.

Without a protest he walked to the class but dragging his feet at it.

As soon as he entered the average sized class he searched for a seat that would be more suited for him.

The varnished brown desk at the back right corner of the class was unoccupied, he decided he would sit there for the whole of the long year he was already in.

The desks were all two-sitters, which meant the pupils in that class were going to sit in pairs. He hated that.

Patrick walked to the desk with his eyes fixed on the brown tiled floor beneath his feet. His gaze was so intensely fixed on the floor you'd swear that he was trying to make on the brown floor the reflection of the white ceiling above - but he was simply avoiding eye contact.

He greeted no one in that class and expected the same from everyone else in return. But as he made his way to the rear corner desk, he heard light footsteps following from behind, they were approaching him. And a voice rather very familiar to Patrick's ears by then came from the person following behind him, "Seems like we beat the odds, huh?" The voice awaited a response, so it sounded. And he needed not to turn to be sure of who it was.

"Yep." He affirmed knowing exactly what she was talking about, "It seems we did." He answered back concealing in his voice the stress that came with beating those particular odds.
He kept moving to the soon to be his desk, and the footsteps kept following closely behind.
By the time he sat down Hannah was already standing beside him. He did not expect it, but wasn't that surprised either when she asked him to make way for she wanted to share the desk with him. He hated the fact that he couldn't refuse her to sit there. And if he was to share his desk it was better to be with her than anyone else.

A couple of minutes later all chairs in Patrick's class were occupied and the same could be said about the other eighth graders' classes as well. The two desk-mates had not had a lengthy conversation yet, simply because Hannah had been busy greeting and catching up with friends from primary school. Friends she was to share her first class of high school with. Patrick did catch sight of a few individuals whom he shared seventh grade with, but like him they too bothered not to greet him. Sharing seventh grade with him made them aware of the kind of person he was, not much of a greeter, let alone a talker.
The teacher who had been calling pupils to their new classes entered Patrick's class and announced herself as Ms. Mathews, she also told the class that she was going to be their class teacher and was going to be the one to teach them the mind-stretching art of numbers that is Mathematics.
Ms. Mathews then asked of the pupils in order of their seats to stand up one by one and state their names, Patrick would be the last, given where he sat in the class.
After thirty learners stood one by one and stated their names it was Hannah's turn to do the same. She stood up and you could see the confidence in her "Hi, my name is Johanna S. Motlhajwa." in an audible voice.

So Hannah wasn't her full name, Patrick chuckled in thought and started thinking about whether he too should say 'hi' before stating his names or not, and if he should state along the first letter of his middle name as the girl beside him had just done. He got lost in his thoughts

yet again that the teacher had to shout 'Next!' staring right at him.
He stood up, held his head upright and began "My name is Patrick." He paused and concluded to say "Patrick Mot." in a firm and audible voice as well. Most of the young girls in his class turned to the sound of his voice and looked at him the same way Hannah looked at him adrift her secret desires, with intrigued eyes, but he would not give them the pleasure of looking back at them.
He sat back down and buried back his head in the small pocket diary with a pen in hand. He was drawing something, for her!
The teacher allowed her pupils a few minutes to properly introduce themselves first to their desk-mates before moving on to nearby desks all the way to the furthest. Hannah did amusingly introduce herself to Patrick whom replied back by saying "I already know." and bothered not to introduce himself to her.
As first time high school scholars moved about in the class introducing themselves to their new classmates Patrick just sat down and kept drawing.
Those who came to introduce themselves to him he neutrally acknowledged without any dismissive behaviour, but his scowl whenever they tried to make small talk would force them to move on.

"Okay back to your seats. Now let's get to know each other even better." She stated adjusting the reading glasses she wore "You are now going to stand one by one in the same manner you did when you stated your names, but this time you are going to tell your class mates what you want to be when you grow up." Said the teacher and pointed at one of the girls who sat at the first desk closest to the door and again in a facilitative tone she said "You there, can you please start."
The learners one by one did as the teacher had asked of them. One after the other they stood and stated most of incredible careers to follow in life.
It got to Hannah. She stood up, and once again with her inviting voice to listen to she began "When I grow up, I want to be a nurse so I could help sick people get better and happy."
Patrick knew that then it was his turn to stand as soon as she sat down and tell the whole class what was it that he wanted to be when he grew up. But like before he drowned in his thoughts and remained seated after Hannah had sat back down.

The fourteen year old at first had wanted to be an astronomer - he was always fascinated by the place beyond the earth, all the stars above at night gave him endless wonders of the place that by then could only be reached by mere sight. He had enjoyed every time every word of his mentor's explanations when they exchanged ideas that had to do with the topic that composed of the suspicions of life beyond Earth, in other words, aliens! But when his mother got sick he changed to desperately wanting to be a medical doctor - only so that he could heal his mother. But when his mother sadly passed away not so long after her diagnosis he knew exactly what was it that he wanted to be when he grew up then.

"Patrick!" Ms. Mathews called out to him. The youngster stood upright and answered back as demanding a question.
Ms. Mathews looked at him and asked "Patrick, would you please tell the whole class what you want to be when you grow up?" She was by then more familiar with his name, and like most teachers by then would've picked up Patrick to be a troublesome kid who pays the least attention in class and gets the lowest scores on tests, she was definitely in for a surprise.
Patrick looked at the teacher and audibly answered to say "When I grow up..." and there again, that pause in his response that seemed to suggest that he was thoughtfully choosing what to say next, "I want to be alive." The whole class started laughing at his response including the girl beside him, but she did so with a bit of confusion as she sought to understand what he meant with such a ridiculous statement. Everyone thought he was exercising his humorous side, but the boy was far from it. Dead serious was what he was.
Even Ms. Mathews smiled a bit, but from Patrick's face she could read that the boy was actually serious, that he intently meant it as he stated it, being alive was the one thing he wanted above all in life. "Patrick, I think you don't understand the question." Said the teacher "You can't choose being alive as something you want to be when you grow up."
Still standing Patrick answered back but with a low voice, "Then you don't understand life yourself." He had intended to keep the response to himself but the words came out anyway and everyone heard. And with the different pitch of voice when saying the words, anyone attentive enough could have read that the emotions attached to the response ran way deep in the boy who preferred to keep his emotions to himself.
He sat back down and when he raised his eyes the whole class was staring at him still, including Ms. Mathews.

Just when the shock stricken teacher was about to say something back in response the bell to break time rang, "Let's pray for the food." She said instead. Had the bell not rung, she would have said something different. 'Saved by the bell' as the saying goes.
The learners went to lunch and came back to class forty five minutes later. No teacher came to Patrick's class for the rest of the day till school out that afternoon. Patrick spent the boring time drawing in his journal and made sure to quickly end every conversation within the first minute of initiation from his desk mate. And Hannah would convince herself that Patrick was in an odd mood that would presently pass, but would later learn that it was not a mood, but rather, his personality!
He never showed her the flower that he drew for her, let alone give it to her.

His whole idea of a first day at a new school was far dissimilar from what he had experienced that day. His primary school days were tolerable because he had Alfred, someone he could have a conversation with without feeling the need to hide his high IQ.
Having to go back to that school the next day, was a drag, and the thought of having to keep going back again and again for the next five years, was the ultimate nightmare of the coldest night, and one that waking up from was not an option
In front of the house lab he reached for one of the two lab coats that were hanged next to the lab door, but he hanged it back before he put it on and thought "I *don't have to wear this today*." and entered the lab.

He pulled on one of the three drawers all labeled 'files', inside it there were two files one labeled 'first theory' and the other 'second theory'. The two files contained each research he's done on his two theories respectively. He did not dwell much into which file to pick, he simply thought "*First comes before second.*" and grabbed the file labeled 'first theory'. He reread what he had written down and accepted December last year as his own first theory in relation to curing the world's common denominator in himself, the fatal flaw in everyone, mortality. His work was past theorizing. In theory he had cured mortality. But time and time again he and Alfred in that very lab had disproven very convincing theories before. So he knew that there was a chance that both theories might not work out to his expectations. For one, there were facts in second theory that suggested that the transplantation of the brain might not actually give immortality, but rather extend the life span of the individual. Because there was nothing in second theory that would stop or at the least slow down cellular degeneration in the brain itself. It was first theory that had more promise to achieving immortality, but it was the most complex of the two theories.

The next four days would be the longest he's ever had. It's only then that his specific test subjects for first theory would arrive. And only then can he start his first experiments of the infinite project so he named it.
Four lizards would be delivered to the house. But not just any regular lizards, these lizards were special. They are one of the few animal species on earth that have mastered the ability of accelerated cellular restoration. Mastered so that they can actually reinstate severed limbs at will and at an amazing speed too. He foresaw having actual fun in these experiments to come that he wished Alfred could be with him in the lab as he conducted them...

Half way through his spaghetti meal that evening the house phone rang. It struck him as rather unusual because no one had ever called that phone since the trial and sentencing of Mr. T.
He rushed to it and answered with a drawn back voice, and then the voice on the other side of the line froze him, *"Son? Is that you?"*
Patrick almost dropped the phone in shock, he could not speak. His heart pounded hard beneath his chest, almost as if trying to break through the chest cavity.
The man on the other side of the line was not a dream, he was as real as it gets. But sadly a different form of disappointment awaited the young man trying his best to hide the fact that he missed his father, and would give anything to have him walk back into his life.
After a few rather long seconds of silence the voice on the other side broke it *"Patrick, it's me, your dad, Alfred, calling from prison."*
Patrick's heart rate started to slow down as he came to understand that it was Mr. T on the other side of the line and not his father, John Mot. Alfred had to maintain the lie that Patrick was his son.
He concealed the confusion he had about the identity of the man on the other side of the line and greeted back asking the man how he was, but he did not address him as his father.
"Not good son." Mr. T replied back *"I'm missing home, and you're the only one I'm allowed to call for you're my son, not that I have anyone else to call. Anyway how's your new school? You like it?"*
Patrick did not want to bore Mr. T with the real boring experience he

had on his first day, he falsified the story instead, told Mr. T what he wanted to hear. He falsely expressed his first day at school as one of the greatest he's ever had…
While the two were deep in conversation, Patrick heard a voice in the background informing Mr. T that his five minutes were done and that he should say his goodbyes. "*Son…*"
Patrick interrupted "Yeah…I heard…you've got to go." Both said their goodbyes and it was Mr. T who hung the phone first, and forgot to ask when Patrick was going to visit him again in prison.

His meal he never finished. He just sat there thinking about his parents and the days when they were both still around, those were his happy days.
Then an idea born of desperation to one more time see both his parents crossed his mind.
Through his days of solitude in his spare time when not working on formulating ways to curing his own mortality he had researched the mysteries around dreams - how do they come about? And why do they come about? A question most people never care to ask, but again, 'he' wasn't 'most' people. His curiosity never depleted with aging as it does with most kids or rather should. Instead, his grew with him.
He had learnt that dreams are the thoughts that run through one's mind during sleep. Those thoughts are most likely the things one fears most or one desires very much. That the last thought through one's mind before sleep was more likely to influence the nature of the dream.
His thirteenth birthday - thirty first August, the year 2011 - the jolliest day of his short lived happy days. Patrick believed if he replayed that day realistic enough in his head he would most likely dream of it, and would surely see his parents in the dream.
He and his parents spent the whole afternoon of that day at MANBEAST PARK, the Roseville's own local amusement park, to celebrate his thirteenth birthday. He spent the afternoon jumping from one ride to another. And when the day was over, back at the house his dad surprised him with a brand new Play Station 2 game console as a birthday gift - it was his first of the new edition.
His mother too got him something, but mothers will always be mothers, super caring they are. She had got him a basket full of sanitary products and the basket had a note that read '*keep clean my son, and remember; mommy loves you.*' typical of a loving and caring

mother, wasn't it?

That day compared to none, but again all his birthdays compared to none and it was all thanks to having had both parents around, too bad that was no more and would never be since both parents were departed; one abducted by death and the other by life itself.

Settled under the light sheet he started to reminisce his thirteenth birthday, the whole afternoon from when he got back from school till the late hours of that night. He fell asleep with the thought of him between his mother and father strolling from the amusement park with the reddish sun setting in the background. The park was not that far away from the Mot residence that they did not have to use a car...

CHAPTER THREE: Hannah's first visit

He woke and turned to the round alarm clock on his bedside table, set to wake him up every morning at five thirty from then on for school. It was only two minutes before the alarm could go off. "Why did I even set it?" He whimpered, as he reached for the alarm clock to turn it OFF in advance and a thought ran his mind *"I guess it doesn't work."*, the technique he had employed at an endeavor to have a dream with both of his parents in it.
Instead, he recalled having a nightmare; where in it he was drowning in crocodiles infested waters. The nightmare felt so real that when the terror woke him up in the middle of the night he was able to then practically taste the water in his mouth. But again, maybe his technique did work, just that not in a way the youngster had hoped for. The research revealed that the dream is influenced by what one feels, and not what one pretends to feel. In fact, the technique had worked. Patrick had dreamt of drowning in crocodiles infested waters, drowning in a way portrayed his loneliness - because there was no one around to help him get out of the water just as there isn't anyone in his life to help him get through a day at most, and the crocodile infested water portrayed the world as a whole itself - it's filled with dangers. The dream in a way had really portrayed Patrick's life - he was alone in a place filled with dangers, too bad he didn't realize it, because only then had he caught up to it he might have sought to find out where he went wrong and have a better chance of success when he tried it again.

He kicked himself out of bed and made it.
By seven thirty, he was leaving the house ready for yet another tedious day of school. He locked the door and tested if it was really locked, his departed mother had taught him that it was much better to be safe rather than sorry. It was those little things that made him from time to time to miss her presence.
His heart started pounding against his chest as soon as he caught sight of who walked up ahead on the street quarter full with school kids heading to Rose-High. It was the girl he shared a desk with in class. Not wanting to talk with her, let alone walk with her again, he slowed down his walking pace. But she would not let him have it his way, "Are you going to drag your feet like that the whole way?" The navy blue skirt with the sky blue shirt uniform went along pretty good with her

skin color, it even brought out the beautiful colors in her eyes, "You don't wanna be late on your second day, or do you?" she asked already stationary for him to catch up.
It was only a matter of time before she asked, "What was that yesterday?" She searched to make eye contact, "You wanting to be 'alive' when you grow up." She added on even when she couldn't find his eyes, a needle in a haystack they were to most.
Patrick gawked at her and realized that she demanded an answer. With his eyes fixed back on the ground he replied "I'd rather not say." and immediately suggested with a lazy tone "Let's talk about something else, shall we?"
They walked the rest of the walk to school with few exchanges of words and all personal questions Hannah asked, he gave similar responses to; it was either 'I'd rather not say' or the straight forward 'I don't want to answer that'. It was those similar responses that made Hannah even more interested to know more about the boy who seemed rather not interested to know more about her, but he did not have to ask her all those questions she did him to know more about her.
Regardless their slow pace the two made it to school just in time.

Second period of the day, Mathematics. Fifteen minutes in and already bored. Hands folded and his head tucked, he fell asleep. But his unacceptable gesture would not go unnoticed. Ms. Mathews asked Hannah who sat next to him to wake him.
Dreams really are a mysterious occurrence, they convince the mind of a false reality, and Patrick was caught in one of those during that Math lesson.
In the dream his departed mother was calling out to him, and being in a dream he was unaware of the fact that his mother had died no more than ten months ago.
He could see her figure in a near distance extending a hand to him, but as he tried to reach to her he started realizing that the distance between them was increasing and her figure was slowly disappearing into the unknown distance far ahead.
He was half asleep and half awake, for he was still in the dream yet could hear the voice that was whispering beside him in provocations to wake him up.
It was at that moment that he realized that he was dreaming and that his chance to see his mother was slipping away with every word

uttered by the person who was waking him up. He woke up with rage in his eyes, and bothered not to mask it. He missed his only chance he's had in a long time to see his dead mother. With a piercing gaze he tilted his head to her, "You have no idea what you've just denied me!" Hannah could clearly see in his eyes that he was angered. She had no idea what was it that he was talking about; what was it that she had denied him by waking him up, and she didn't even ask, simply because she didn't like how he snapped at her, and would prefer not to talk to him for the rest of the day hoping it would lead him to realize his fault and apologize. But that was exactly what Patrick hoped for from her - a break from her inquisitive questions.

He faced his front and found Ms. Mathews staring at him along with majority of his classmates. He apologized, for sleeping in class, but he didn't really mean it, he actually thanked sleeping in class for it gave him that one chance to see and feel the presence of his mother, even just for those few seconds it was enough to elicit hope of once again seeing his mother in 'dreamland'.

The lesson continued, but Patrick took no part in it, he pretended to be trying to solve the math problems like everyone else was doing, but he wasn't. He was actually trying to figure out what had triggered the dream, but nothing came to mind and chances were it wasn't going to come at all. And Math problem on the board, he had already solved in his head yet had zero desires to share his solution or show how he got his solve with everyone in his class who seemed to be drifting further away from the answer with every guess attempt at the answer.

Break time after the third period. The very same secluded tree he had leaned against the previous day.

The chattering masses a fair distance away, he could not make out their words; all he could hear from where he stood were buzzes. The tree was perfect for him, he'd definitely eat tomorrow's lunch at that tree, and the many to follow after that, he decided.

He kept watching as individuals making groups of classmates and friends interacted with each other, something he has never been part of, a group of friends. The only type of fun he's ever had in his life was playing video games with his father or at times teaming up with his older version to tease his mother. Visiting the MANBEAST Park was also much preferred and in some afternoons when Mr. T would be in some teacher's convention which he attended at the least once a week Patrick would formulate his own experiments which he never shared with his mentor. Speed riding his bike round Roseville was also one of his pleasurable activities. The youngster had never looked at another seeking to have a good or fun time, his imagination alone was enough company.

After break time two lessons came and passed, each taught by a different teacher. The third and last period of the day it was Natural Sciences', by far Patrick's favorite subject with mathematics seconding it at times.
The Natural Sciences' teacher entered the class and announced himself as Sir Jackson - he started the lesson right away saying he'd learn all their names as he goes along. But he would not hesitate to ask his first question to the freshmen.
"Say you were asked, 'What is…the basic unit of life?', what would you say?" he asked invitingly so to stimulate a vast variety of responses, in hopes that one of those responses will be the correct answer, "And how would you say this basic unit of life leads to the higher functional plants and animals we see all around us?" he added on.
The teacher's inviting self-presentation worked, hands were raised and opinions were shared. Amused by the responses, even Patrick laughed with a smiled at most of the thoughts that were shared. He knew the correct answer from the moment the question was asked, of which the teacher had not yet got from the dozens of freshmen who raised their hands, some confident, others hesitant, and others close enough to the answer, but wrong all alike still.
Even when other's raised their hands for the second even third time at an attempt at the correct answer, Patrick would still not raise his.
It was when he frowned at a few frivolous guesses from his class mates that Sir Jackson knew that the silent kid at the back had something different to say. But he would not ambush him by asking him directly.
"Young lady at the back…" the teacher called out to Hannah, "Wanna take another guess?"
She would not refuse a second chance to appear smart on her second day of high school. When she answered that 'oxygen' was the basic unit of life Patrick whispered making sure she'd be the only one to hear him. But the secretly observant teacher saw his mouth work, "Seems like your neighbor has something to say." He said, "What did he say to you?" he asked Hannah, whom easily revealed that Patrick had said that she was wrong, again!
"Okay, why don't you tell us what you think…" it was more of a

suggestion to Patrick than a request, this one teacher knew his way with words - he was perfect for the freshmen. So far no one in Patrick's class had given him the correct answer, yet no one thought any less of themselves. That's how good he was at stimulating participation.

With a firm voice, Patrick replied, but not with the answer, rather with a question, "What was the question, again?" he asked and his voice did that thing again, where it grabbed every girl's attention in that class. And when the teacher rephrased his two questions as he had first and time again before, Patrick began with his eyes fixed on the top surface of his desk, "The basic unit of all life is a cell." He was audible enough. When the teacher nodded in agreement even the boys turned their attention to him wanting to hear what more he had to say. He raised his eyes to the teacher and continued "The parent cell multiplies into more cells creating different colonies of cells or tissues, the different tissues then form different organs, groups of these organs form systems, and when these systems work together it's then that you get a higher functional and later a reproductive organism like the plants and animals we see all around us." He folded his hands on his desk and pressed his chin against his wrist, but kept looking at the teacher. When Sir Jackson kept nodding and said that in all the four correct answers he got from five classes that day, Patrick's answer was definitely the most elaborate; his class mates clapped their hands for him. But he would not bask in any of it.

Patrick had learned things that were two grades ahead of him on most of the topics covered in Natural Sciences, unconsciously feeding his curious mind and improving his intellect for the better, a higher intellect he rarely admitted to having.

School out, at least one thing wasn't a drag, he agreed. He had enjoyed the NS lesson. And there was an underlying reason to it, John Mot. His father was the one who introduced him to the basic units of life, cells. Stalling, he slowly packed his books into his backpack; he wanted to walk home alone with fewer kids on the streets.

Just when at the doorway ready to leave, the teacher who had also hanged back stopped him to ask "Son, what's your name?"

"Patrick." He answered, "It's Patrick, sir." Having turned to the teacher he repeated and stood as upright as he could.

He wanted to add in his last name but the teacher beat him to the first word, "Patrick huh! Let me guess..." He appeared to be trying to remember a name when he paused to say "There's only one Patrick

that comes to my mind who fits your first impression today perfectly and that is...Mot, Patrick Mot." Then the teacher asked "Are you by any chance that 'Patrick'? Patrick Mot I mean."
How could he have known? He wondered, he wasn't that popular in primary school, so how could he have known? His need to know bugged his interest, "Yes sir, I am." He paused before revealing his interest, "And how do you know that, sir? If I may ask that is."

"Your father." He said, "That man tells me a lot about you, I might even say that I knew you way before I knew you."
Was he dreaming in class, again? He questioned and inspected secretly by biting on his tongue. When he would not wake up, he asked "You talk to my dad?" He hoped for an affirmative response from the small headed teacher who looked no atypical to the type of men who are found in his line of work. Neat, suggesting that there's a wife back home who takes good care of him, but that might not be the case as Mr. T lived the life of a solitary bachelor detached from his family. He had a woman in his life, once. They eloped into Roseville to get married. Alfred's father had looked him dead in the eye and said; no son of his would marry a white woman, and that if he did...he would no longer be his son...
"Not exactly 'talk'." The teacher answered to explain "More like writing to him and he's been writing back. He asked me to keep an eye on you should you be in any of my classes. Says you're the only one he's allowed to talk to through arranged visits, or on the phone." He added immediately "Strict 'prison laws'." It's then that Patrick realized that sir Jackson was not talking about his father, Mr. Mot, but that he was instead talking about Mr. T who's in prison. Had Sir Jackson been in Mr. T's trial Patrick would've known from the beginning who he was talking about.
The conversation was no longer interesting to him, and he would not bother hide it.
Sir Jackson could not hold him against his will, so as soon as he noticed his lack of interest he had to let him go, "Okay then, see you tomorrow Patrick." He said, he too said the same back and left the class...

Remembering that he wouldn't be home during the early hours of Friday, he grabbed first his laptop. He had to notify the pet company he had ordered the lizards from to deliver them late in the afternoon; he'd surely be back from school then. And before he could change out of his school uniform, there was a knock at the front door.

He opened the door, and as soon as he saw who it was behind it, he lowered his eyes, he tended to do that; avoid making eye contact with anyone. "Oh! The home-work." He recalled and invited her in "*Is it me or does she get prettier every time I see her...*" he thought.
Sir Jackson had partnered each learner with another in reference to how close they lived to one another. In that manner, Patrick was partnered with Hannah for all the Natural Sciences' activities to be completed in pairs that year.
"I'll just go change...be back in a bit." He said after showing her where to sit in the TV room.
"Be quick, we've got a lot to do." She urged him on and by then it seemed she had looked past the morning incident in class.
Looking around she was impressed and stood corrected. She had imagined how untidy the house would be given that it was run by a teenage boy living alone with no one to remind him of the house chores he had to do.

It was only a few minutes before Patrick walked back into the TV room barefooted.
Sir Jackson had asked each pair to choose one topic around the chapter 'Earth and Beyond' to study and present to the class the following day during Natural Sciences' period.
Patrick had already decided for both him and Hannah to do the presentation on the topic 'Life beyond Earth', all he had to do then was to convince her to agree to it.
"As long as you..." She quickly paused to correct herself "I mean as long as we've got enough facts to accompany the topic...then I guess we can do our presentation on 'aliens'." Her tone was acknowledging as it was mocking, she didn't know much about aliens other than her 'fact' that they didn't exist. But would funny enough one of these days call Patrick one.
He stood and asked to be excused. When he walked back into the TV room he had with him a file that he extended to her, "Will these be enough facts?" He asked and bravely dared to take a brief glance into her eyes.
"So you have already done it!" She exclaimed then asked "When did you do it?"
When he answered he couldn't be wrong, it was just a couple of weeks before the passing of his mother.
"These are enough facts alright, but it would be cheating to present this

in class tomorrow." For a moment she was able to look back into his eyes and only because he let her, "Patrick we have to actually do the research...plus they are going to laugh at us for believing in the existence of aliens, don't you think?"
"Yeah, you're right." he said, "So what's the new topic?" he asked and quickly added "And one they won't laugh at us when we present."...

Later that night the young Mot slept on the couch with the television ON, but since he had actually planned on sleeping on the couch he made sure to bring his alarm clock into the TV room...
The alarm clock rang at five thirty in the morning just as it had been set to, and that time he did not wake before it. It had actually pulled him out of a dream. For the first time he experienced things boys his age did. One of those dreams that one wakes up from with a smile and the burning desire to start over the whole dream - there were even drools all over the pillow he had rested his head over. It was his first wet dream, the first of many to follow.

Third period of the day just before lunch was NS' again! And they impressed Sir Jackson even more than Patrick had solely done the previous day.
They took harmonized turns in presenting their poster. They even asked their audience - their classmates - simple little follow up questions to check if they were listening attentively and to keep them interested in what they had to say. And they had a lot to say about their solar system.
It is said that the best is saved for last; and with their presentation and they being the last pair to present, that saying was perfectly supported. They got full marks yet the teacher's praise and the applause of their audience suggested that they deserved even more. Hannah couldn't be happier. But when she turned to Patrick who should share the joy for their triumph, she rather met with the usual destitute expression on his face. First thought to be a phase, she was slowly learning otherwise and would soon learn to accept it as who he was.
"Come on Patrick! Smile a little." She said, and when he would not smile she added, "You're strange!" yet she would not imagine him different, because his strangeness was strangely what she liked about him.
Giving her that scowled look and flexing on his jaw muscles he worked his mouth to say something, but he did not. He just stood there next to her before their peers with his hands tucked away behind his back like

a young soldier before a high ranked commanding officer. Yep! This boy was strange.

Friday morning - Patrick couldn't wait to get home from school and wait for the delivery of the lizards that afternoon. He even left early for school.
Even in class, one attentive enough could have notice that he was impatient. And his impatience only made him think that time was awfully moving slowly that day.
When the school out bell rang he did not wait for the crowd to disperse first. But not wanting to walk amongst a crowd still, he rushed to walk ahead of them instead.

After two long hours of waiting, finally! The white delivery truck with animal decorations and the pet company logo on the sides came to stop in front of the gate, and honked the horn.
Patrick walked out the house's front door with the front gate keys in hand. He opened the gate and the van got through in reverse, making that beeping sound no different to that of bigger delivery trucks when in the similar reverse motion.
A few meters from the house it stopped, and a white man came out the driver's side, seemingly in a hurry he greeted, "Good day!"
He was tall, the tallest Patrick had ever seen by far. His head was suspended on a thin body, and had one of those faces you see in western movies - folks with funny mustaches stretching across over their upper lips, sometimes even going all the way round their mouths. All that was left out to complete his cowboy look was the typical hat of Wild West men. But the black hair mixed in with the grey few on his head did not make him appear any less of a gun slinger who would have lived in the Western United States during its frontier period.
Before he could unload what he had delivered, he asked Patrick for any of his parents and was surprised, when he learnt that it was Patrick who had actually placed the order. There being no policy against that he had no grounds to refuse him purchasing the lizards.
He showed Patrick the cargo and asked if it was precisely what he had ordered to purchase. Looking at the four lizards inside a one by one meter glass tank of half a meter height with its inside decorated so to mimic their natural habitat he noted "Two adults and two on the young side, yeah, this is exactly what I ordered, wait..." He paused with evident perplexity in his eyes, face and voice alike "How do I tell which are males and which are females?" he asked.

It was actually simple, the man explained, the males' necks were dark brown while the females' were purplish.

The two, Patrick and the deliveryman, picked up the tank and carried it into the house moving with caution as to not scare the lizards. Patrick saw it fit to place the tank in the lab. He had hidden away most of the material that would hint his intentions with the lizards. He would not be allowed to make the purchase if animal cruelty was even slightly suspected.
The two came back to the van, took all necessary equipments, which included lights that will play the role of sunlight and temperature regulators since the lizards were going to live indoors. The tank came with water pipes already installed in it. They made the hydration process much easier. He even received an instruction book on everything about having those kinds of lizards for pets, from how to regulate the lights' brightness and temperature, when to feed them, when to make it rain and so on. But all the youngster was interested in was their ability to regenerate damaged or lost cells at will and at an accelerated rate too. He had no interests in their wellbeing, and ultimately cared not for their survival, 'yet'. Even when he had to change his plan of starting his experiments on the lizards the following day, to next week Saturday; it was a calculated logical move. He did that to allow the lizards enough time to get used to their new environment. He had previously learnt that a lizard generally responds much better to any stimulus in relation to the mood it's in. So in his case he had to trick and make the lizards feel at home so that they would not be shy to show off their capabilities when the time to experiment comes...

Seven days passed - Friday afternoon - Patrick had already with the aid of the manual book, gained the trust of the lizards to a point that he was then able to put any of the two young fifteen centimeter lizards on his hand and it would not attempt to get away.
Realizing that it had been a while since he had last seen the female adult, he stood up and retrieved a flashlight from one of the drawers in the lab. He squatted back beside the tank and shown the light in the dark area where the lizards hide away when they've had enough of the skin warming light.
Curdled in the shadows looking back at him there it was. And just when he was to turn off the penlight after confirming that the lizard was okay, it moved a little, and beneath its belly he could clearly see

them, eggs! It had been scarce because it has been busy incubating the eggs it had laid no more than two days ago. He bought it pregnant. Quickly he turned OFF the light and stood away from the tank. He would not want 'her' believing that he posed a danger to 'her' eggs. Even though Patrick did not admit it, in the last seven days he had grown fond of the lizards and seeing the egg incubation, made him question his plans to cut the lizards up, like lab rats. As soon as he had questions he had resolves too.
The life expectancy of the specific lizards he had was a decade, and the oldest amongst the four he had was only three years old - which meant that he could halt his experiments for the next six years if he wanted to and halt them he did without even debating it. His decision an impulse born of emotions he himself did not understand, or rather have felt before. Patrick had never owned a pet before.

Saturday morning - just at the crack of dawn - after having a morning meal of oats he locked himself inside the lab. Cleaned what was on the white board and at the top of it, right in the middle he wrote 'the other me'.
Minutes later, and he still couldn't come up with anything solid. Whenever he wrote an idea he erased it immediately after reading it aloud to himself and realizing how stupid and impractical it sounded. The wrist digital watch on his right wrist started beeping, "Oh, it's food time for you guys." He said turning to the tank, and left the lab half an hour later still without a façade to mask the strange person he was. It seemed even he admitted that he was too strange, yet wouldn't change it, but would at the least learn to hide it...

Monday morning, halfway to school, there she was, walking alone on the sidewalk of the street cuddling a couple of textbooks in her hands. "Hey you..." He greeted first, she greeted back and the two began to walk together at a much slower pace compared to the one Hannah had been walking at alone.
Patrick maybe did not realize it, but his voice when he talked with her then was different to his usual low drawn back tone. He was even the inquisitive one, and when she too asked him question he made sure to answer them all without protest, or the usual 'I'd rather not say'. But it shouldn't have counted for anything for most responses were falsified in parts. He made up stories straying from the truth hoping to appear less strange and weird.
She so wanted to ask him why was he so talkative all of the sudden, but

feared it might only cause him to revert back to his drawn back self. Only a few meters from the school gate, Patrick ended "Time sure flies when you're in a conversation." She would not disagree yet did not voice her agreement. She could not help but wonder why he was so different all of the sudden.

"You do like drawing, don't you?" She asked when she noticed that it was the first thing he attended to after settling down.
"No! I don't think so." He answered briefly, and when she asked why he does it so often then, he explained without pausing his drawing "It helps me relax, plus there's nothing I feel I'd rather do right now." he spoke slowly and shrugged his shoulders at the end.
Her eyes slowly following the trimmed edge of his darker hair back to his ear then she murmured "But doesn't preferring something over another mean you like it?"
"Not really." He answered, and when he turned to her he avoided her eyes "I've seen you take notes almost in every period, does that mean you like taking notes?" he asked.
"Of course not." She answered, "I just prefer to have them in hand when I need them, better safe than sorry, you know!" He knew, way more than she realized. That phrase; 'better safe than sorry.' His mother used to say that.
"See!" he retorted "You don't like it, yet you prefer to do it. case closed!" the smug on his face as he made the point.

The first teacher to class came a bit late - it was during that lesson that Patrick did something no one expected from the 'silent boy' at the rear desk.
While the Social Sciences' teacher was exchanging opinions with the learners on the harsh character 'Adolf Hitler' played during his dictatorship years, the boy, Patrick, exposed the dictator's methods to ridicule one too many times and the class laughed at the mocking of the tyrant, doing so they only riled him up to do it some more. The behavior overlapped into other periods as well, except math, there's nothing to joke about in math except the fact of how many learners actually fail it.
By the next day, Patrick had already won the acknowledgement of a whole lot of his classmates, boys and girls alike, as the funniest. Then it hit him; maybe that was his façade - the dark kid, marked by an intense ridiculing predilection, the class clown…

CHAPTER FOUR: A hand's reach away

Four years since his freshman year, August - twelfth grade - Patrick had precisely chosen this year and month to begin his experiments on the lizards, in hopes of having a testable serum by the end of that very year, before having to start 'second theory' that same year.
Thursday morning in class, he wouldn't keep his eyes off of her for a stretched interval. A beautiful young woman by then, not his yet - she still lived across Mr. T's house.
"*What do I stand to lose?*" he thought as he stood up and headed straight for her desk.
The two had been in different classes from ninth grade, but then in twelfth grade, they were once again in the same class. But unlike in their first year of high school, they did not share a desk. And he wanted to change that, since the first day in that class when he realized that they'd share it.
Mere meters from her desk one of her friends beat him to it, they started a girl talk. Quickly, he made it seem as if he was never headed for her desk, but for the rubbish bin instead - he threw a piece of paper he balled up in his fist into the bin in the front corner and turned away only to stare at her from a distance still. He would not speak his intents with her in the presence of another.
His plan was to wait for the perfect moment, when she's all alone and ask her in the nicest way he could to come sit next to him for the rest of the year. He knew chances were he was never going to sit next to her again in his life; they were already in their last five months of high school.

When he sat back down, he took out his drawing book and started spinning his pen around his fingers trying to think of what to draw. Back in eighth grade he had told her that drawing helped him to not think a lot, but that was false. The truth was that it helped him to relax and released his mental pressure, thus making his thinking less stressful. It made it that much easier for him to come up with solutions to any practical and thinkable problems he might have in that moment. So in other words, drawing actually helped him to think a lot, just at ease. And it still did.
He paid much attention to his drawing, but the moment her loud mouthed, talkative friend moved away from her desk he noticed, so did

everyone else. What the small headed Veronica slightly lacked in intellectual capacity, she made up for in personality and stature. Boldly high built and never feared speaking her mind. She and Hannah had been the best of friends since primary school. Unfortunately the only class of high school they got to share was their final, but would surely unlike most, remain friends after high school.

The moment was right, perfect even, for his plan. Up on his feet again he approached. But midway he stopped, and had she not turned to see him, he would've turned back. But it was now too late for that. Their eyes met, and for the first time in a long while he maintained the eye contact and quickly thought to himself *"There's no turning back from it now."* He approached.
He leaned in, and just when he was that close to her face and able to smell the scent of her perfume on her skin he began "Hey…can I ask you something?" his voice more thicker now.
"Yeah…go ahead." Ever smiling she affirmed, "Not that you needed to ask for permission, Patrick!"
"Can you come sit next to me at the back, for the rest of the year?" He asked, "Plus, you'd have a better view of the class and the board…I've seen how you struggle to see the notes on the board."
"No, I can't." She turned him down, and tried her best to keep a straight face while hoping that he could not see how red she turned. "I think I'll be fine right here for the rest of the year." But the burning desire to say yes was heating her up from the inside, and soon, a blushing smile would curl.
"Okay." he stood back straight and fiddled first with the strap on his wrist watch, "I guess it's back to staring at you from a distance." He said, and slowly turned to walk away.
Spontaneously, she reached for his hand but grabbed the end bit of his black belt. She quickly drew back her hand as the belt somehow resembled a snake in her hand "Wait!" And when he turned to look into her face she shied her eyes away and asked "You can't give up so easily…Aren't you gonna try to convince me to agree?" it was simply one of those moments where a lady's 'no' meant a 'yes'. She just wanted to hear him work for it, but he would not play that game, he would play his own.
"Not really." He answered not even bothering to find her eyes, "I'm trying to respect your choice." He walked away. A master manipulator he had turned into and he knew it, for he learnt it, taught himself it. But

rarely used it.
Lessons started on the second period for the Life Sciences' teacher was absent from school, and would be for the whole of that week due to a sudden illness. All the classes she taught were made aware of her absence in that week...

Back in the lab he had replaced the old tank with a larger one. And he had to, for he had nine lizards in total then.
The adults bred only two lizards and the other two lizards came into adulthood and bred three more lizards, bringing the total number of lizards to nine. None had died, thanks to their ability to quickly regenerate lost cells, which meant their aging process was much slower when compared in proportion with other lizards.
"Hey guys..." Over the years he's come to treat them like pets for real instead of test subjects to be experimented on as he intended to, "Who wants an arm ride?" He asked putting his hand through the hatchway on the lid of the tank - the lid made the roof.
He pulled out his hand and raised his wrist still with the lizard on his hand, much closer to his face, he whispered to it "Don't worry...I won't do it." He said "First doesn't always have to come before second."
And that was it - the emotions that caused him to halt the experiments four years ago have been growing inside him. And now that they have grown they were slowly taking over the helm.
After feeding his now 'pets' and changing their drinking water he left the lab, but let it rain in the tank for several minutes first.
It was not long during his home-works when he decided to call the Roseville's own pet store, and inquire about giving away all the nine lizards he had.
By late afternoon the lizards were gone, all of them, as well as all the equipments they came with. The only proofs that lizards were ever harbored in the house laboratory for more than four years were his memories of his scaled friends.
He did not really know why he did it. All he knew was that they would have a better home, where they can be fully taken care of.
Watching the truck drive away was unpleasant to him, he could only describe the feeling as similar to the one he felt back when his mother dropped him off for his first day of primary school and drove away leaving him there 'alone'...

Friday morning, he left the house for school at exactly seven thirty. Like always; he locked the door and checked if it was locked by

attempting to open it without unlocking it. When he got out the yard walking not that far away in front of him was Hannah, but she was not by herself. She was with Veronica and a couple more of their other friends.
He had to decide whether to walk slower behind them or walk faster as to walk past them. But walking slower would see him risking being late by a few minutes if not more, an act which was not tolerated when it came to seniors doing their final year.
He increased his walking pace and walked past them without greeting. But Veronica would not let him walk past just like that, "So you gonna just walk past us like we're not human beings?" and when she went unanswered she added "That's why you don't have any friends, Mot!" Even though Hannah wanted to tell her friend how rude of her that was, she knew there was truth in it, and Patrick had it coming, he should learn to greet people, she debated in her head. She was by then used to how Patrick treated her when she's around her friends, or anyone for that matter. She was a complete stranger to him, whenever she had company that is. And sometimes would even wish they were not around so much, preferred those little conversations she had with him whenever it was just the two of them.

Before even delivering her backpack, she made her way towards Patrick's desk, definitely to talk about what Veronica had said to him on the road.
Meeting his raised eyes she greeted first, and when he revealed that he held nothing against what Veronica had said to him, probably because even he knew it was true, Hannah took off her backpack and rested it on top of his desk, "You were right." she said, "The board is much clearer from here." And asked "Why didn't you tell me this earlier in the year, Patrick?"
"You seemed pretty attached to that small headed friend of yours and she to you." He retorted and now she could tell that he held something against what Veronica had said to him, "I doubt she would've liked it that much if you had agreed to sit back here."
"Say we find out for sure..." she suggested and added "But you'll have to help me with my assignments and other school stuff if I sit back here, especially math and life sciences and physics of course, deal?"
"Okay, deal!" he said, "I get the desk, and you get the chair."
Immediately they headed her desk's way.
All the desks in twelfth grades of Roseville-High were small one-sitter

desks - only sixty centimeters wide with a forward reach of forty five centimeters and a height of eighty five centimeters from the floor, but the chairs varied in sizes.
Since they've reunited in terms of sharing a class she had wanted to sit next to him again just as he did, but she wouldn't show it, seems it all went back to the primitive norm of the boy having to make the first move, and he did. But too much time had passed already.
The class stared as the two carried the furniture across the class. And surprisingly 'Vero' as her friends called her was first to comment "I knew you were planning on making a move on her, Mot." She always addressed people by their last names, and had nothing to do with the courteous manner of respect. "I knew something was hiding behind that silence." She added. But again all she would get back from him was his silence.
They set the table and chair next to Patrick's, but first had to ask the back dwellers to make space for the new tenant. The two were once again sitting only a hand reaches away from each other.
"What now?" He thought as he awkwardly faced his front with his head held high. And before he could decide what he was to do next, that he had gotten her to sit next to him, she turned to him and began with a radiant smile "It's been a while since we've sat like this." and asked "It brings back old memories, doesn't it?" She still rocked the same hair style, a braided ponytail. Her skin still bright as it has always been, caramel toned it was, the only difference was the developmental changes that came with the process of passage through her adolescent stage. A fine specimen she was growing into, she wouldn't walk by without any boy looking her way.

"It sure does." Patrick affirmed, "I still remember it like it was just yesterday that we were in eighth grade."
He pushed his chair close to hers, so close that the two chairs touched. He leaned in and said to her "I've really missed this." But quickly objected "No..." and only to correct "I mean I've really missed you." He even made a brief but deep eye contact with her that time around to suggest that he was meaning what he was saying.
He attempted to hold her by the waist as they were seated, but held the back of her chair instead and questioned his actions in thought *"What am I doing?"* Something sure was going on in his head, something new or old, but was surely the first time he was acting upon it.

"You, Patrick? Missed me?" She was shocked, and found it hard to believe, "Really?" She questioned his statement but not for confirmation, she knew from the look he gave her alone that he meant what he had just said. But just couldn't bring herself to believe that it was the same Patrick he knew saying it, maybe that was it, maybe it wasn't the same Patrick she knew.

He turned his eyes to her again and as he was about to say something to her she beat him to it, by saying "I'll be right back." She stood up and walked to her friend, whom seemed to be taking the move bad just as they had thought she would.

He knew he only had a few minutes to prepare his speech before she came back to sit down. Patrick wanted to tell her of his life's work so far and the whole goal behind it, and eventually tell her of the nurse post he had in mind for her, exclusively 'her' and no one else. In his head it was either her or no one at all to play the nurse in the final stages of his 'project', the infinite project. But telling her of the 'infinite project' as he called it meant he might actually have to get straight with her, all the lies he had told her in the past he'd have to correct. And he knew the risk of telling someone the truth, you can never be sure of how they'd react. But it was a risk he was willing to take, after all you miss all hundred percent of the shots you don't take.

After the last lesson of the day, Patrick's class was yet again divided into two groups; one that was cleaning that week and the other that would clean the next - they had been alternating cleaning turns in that manner since year start and they planned to keep working that way till year end for every Friday spring-cleaning.

Patrick and Hannah were on the same group - the group that was not cleaning that week.

He took the teacher's desk from his class and went to sit on top of it under a tree shade outside - the desk had the same forward reach and height as any other desk in the class, the only difference was that it was a meter wide. Patrick normally used that time of any Friday when free from cleaning his class even when it was his turn, to plan how he'll go about conducting 'first theory' experiments. But since he had decided to halt 'first theory', he was to use that time to plan his first 'second theory' experiment.

The good news was that 'second theory' was not as complex as 'first theory' was. The key idea of the whole theory was to 'decapitate, reattach and resurrect' the test subject.

The bad news was that he had no test subjects, 'lab rats' in other words. He would need to order another type of pets and subject them to those experiments in 'second theory', but will risk growing fond of them like he did with his last, the lizards, which in turn might cause him to halt 'second theory' as well, he couldn't afford that.
As those ideas ran through his mind he found a resolve for any risk of failure "Zero risk." He said. He decided that he would not purchase any pets. Instead, he would take the bad with the goods, in other words he would make 'lemonades from lemons' that are constantly thrown at him.
There are cats and dogs that get through the fencing at Mr. T's and run around in the yard at night leaving behind only 'crap' in the grass and in the morning he's the one who has to remove it.
His plan was to find a way to capture the dogs and cats without bringing any physical harm to them and subject them to those experiments - in that case he would not have 'lab rats' but 'lab dogs' and 'lab cats' instead, and having only to keep the animal for a few days before an experiment would not serve as enough time for him to develop any intense emotions of fondness towards the animals, so he believed.

Hannah came to stand on the outside corner of her class and caught sight of Patrick a few meters away under the tree shade on the teacher's desk, she immediately walked to him.
"Hey, you like being alone, don't you? And why even." She asked and settled herself comfortably on the desk, but to him she was too close that it unsettled his comfort.
"Actually I don't like it...it's just that I have to do it." He responded closing the book he's been scribbling in, and tried to hide his terrors as her skirt slightly pulled up revealing her bare thigh that she without even realizing pressed gently again his, or didn't she?

That, them sitting together alone served as a chance for him to tell her what he was trying to tell her early morning in class, but he did not. For some reason only known to him he figured it was not a good idea after all. Thought that time best suited to tell her of the reason he asked her to come sit next to him will come. Time best suited for him to tell her truth from all the lies he had to keep up all those years, but what time was better the present? And the sooner he told her the sooner she'd forgive him, if she would.

Conversing with her got easier as he went along with it regardless her nearness. She was the one doing most of the talking. She only kept talking and didn't mind it because she felt listened to. And when she asked if she could ask personal questions, he told her that he would only answer the ones he would feel comfortable answering because he did not want to lie to her just to satisfy her with an answer. In a way he was trying to tell her that there are times he's falsified responses to her.

With his permission, she did not hesitate to ask "Do you have a girlfriend, Patrick?" but the question was rather to confirm than to seek out unknown knowledge. The question Hannah already knew the answer to, she just wanted to hear it from the horse's mouth. After all, she's been living opposite him for over four years then. Had there been any girlfriend she would've seen her by then.

When he answered with an unflinching 'no', she asked again "Why not though? Are you too shy or too scared?" There was a bit of humor in her tone, mocking.

"No." He answered to both, "I'm too busy for that, and even if I had the time, I bet no one would accept the actual person I am. Only my old man does." He said to her with his eyes fixed on his feet dangling close to the ground, "You of all people know how I have no social skills, nor the desire to acquire them. I'd be a very boring boyfriend."

He referred to Mr. T when he said 'my old man'; even Hannah had this idea that Mr. T was Patrick's dad. Patrick had relayed the falsified story of his upbringing to her back in early eighth grade. He had told her that his mother left his dad when he was still young - when he was just starting elementary school and was raised solely by his dad. His dad who was arrested for multiple tax evasions in the late months of the year prior to the one Patrick did his eighth grade. At least he did not lie about the whereabouts of Mr. T and why he's there, but that shouldn't justify the rest of which most was a lie with smaller lies told again and again to cover it up.

"But how would you know that for sure if you don't let people know you?" she asked, "You never make conversation with anyone in class for more than five minutes. You're not even in any of the study groups we have. So how would you know that people won't accept the person you are?" she paused, looked into his even toned dark face and added with a blushing smile "I think you'd make a cool boyfriend."

"Like I said," he interjected "I have no social skills, nor do I have the desire to acquire them." he stopped dangling his feet and rested them

on the bar that connected the front legs of the desk, and asked "What about you? Do you have a boyfriend?" and like her, he already knew the answer to that, he had seen her with him plenty of times.
"Yes, I have a boyfriend." She answered, "And don't act like you haven't seen him, I've caught you staring at us a lot of times from your house already, his name is Kgomotso by the way." She had started dating with him when she was in tenth grade and he was in eleventh grade. Then that she was doing her final year, he had completed high school. He still lived in Roseville. With rich parents to depend on he saw no use of furthering his studies for a career.
"So do you like…love him love him?" he asked, and for some reason murmured lowly to mock "Whatever that means."
"Duh!" Almost rolling her eyes at him "He wouldn't be the boyfriend if I did not…'love him love him'." She answered, her tone suggested that she believed what she was saying, "You do know you gonna be in a relationship one day, right? You won't be an *alien* forever, you know?"

"That I already know. It's inevitable, I've read, even believed to be an 'impulse' primeval rather than a choice calculated and taken." He said, and looked up at the green leafed canopy of the big tree above "I even wonder sometimes, how it would all feel like." he actually intended to just think the last part to himself.
"Inevitable…primeval, I have never heard those words before." she retorted with that face that said she was equally confused as she was interested in what he had to say, "Can you please tell me what they mean, so I could know what you're talking about." She requested and dared to find his eyes.
Dusty brown eyes closely looked into hers, "Inevitable." He began by echoing himself, "It simply means incapable of being avoided or prevented, say growing old and dying. It can't be avoided or prevented '*now*', can it?" the pause he made before saying 'now'! He aimed to defy the inevitable, and hadn't told her, yet. "Primeval means something that has existed from the beginning." And when he looked that long into her eyes he had to say it, softly and slowly "Your eyes are very beautiful!" still looking deeply into them, he neared his head in, slowly still.

She instinctively closed her eyes, and waited anxiously to feel his lips soft and light on hers. "Don't close them." he said, "I want to see what color they actually are."
And when she opened her eyes, for the first time she found his face

uncomfortably close to hers.
Embarrassed at her willingness to kiss the boy who gazed at her passionately without even realizing it, she had to change the topic of her eyes and hopefully get some distance between their faces.
"Enough about my eyes." she said, "You said you sometimes wonder how it would all feel like, what did you mean?" she asked, this topic she did not want to drop.

"This whole...relationship thing." he answered back just after pulling his head back, "I wonder how it would all feel like." He repeated.
Looking ahead just as he was she began "Well, you gonna keep wondering if you don't do something about it." she turned to him and he to her, when he would not shy his eyes away from her, the thought of kissing him invaded her passionate desires again, she glanced briefly at his lips and added with an even face "Find someone you really like and spend time with them, and before you know it, the two of you will be '*kicking-it-off*'." Envy slowly swooped in, because deep down she wanted to be that one person Patrick could really like and grow to love.
But he already did, yet even he didn't suspect it.
"But first I have to learn a few social skills, don't you think?" he asked and turned to look idly into the space ahead, "Too bad they don't teach those here in Rose-High."

The bell to school out rang and the gates were opened for pupils to go home. Then Hannah gave a reply where Patrick did not expect one nor required one, "I can teach you. Maybe even help you find out what it feels like to be in a relationship." Finally, a clue that better proved that she was interested if not attracted to Patrick, and it has been either one of those since she first learnt and caught sight of the boy who lived opposite her new home. Back then Hannah had asked her aunt of Patrick, and the aunt told her niece the little she knew - that the boy only visited on daily basis till he came to live there permanently after his supposedly father was arrested, yep, the aunt too knew nothing about Mr. T other than that he was a school teacher. And with Patrick's daily visits she only insinuated that the school teacher was the father of the boy. And when Mr. T was arrested and Patrick came to live there permanently she again insinuated that the 'son' had come to look after his father's house.
Before Patrick could say anything back Hannah stood and walked away to the class. Leaving Patrick puzzled under the tree shade, and when he saw her follow out her friends his instinct told him to run to her, but he

would not do so. She turned her head to him and waved goodbye, he just nodded back. He would sit there for a few more minutes before deciding to head home as well…

How well the lab coat fitted him then, a young scientist he looked like in it indeed. When Mr. T bought it for him all those years ago, it was a bit large for Patrick. Alfred always excused his failure to get his measurements right at that time by saying that he bought a larger lab coat on purpose so that he wouldn't have to buy him another one when the young lad came of age.
But right then when he was about to unlock the door, there was a knock at the front door.
Hand at the door knob "Who is it?" he asked and wondered how could he have left the gate unlocked last night.
"It's me, Patrick." said the person behind the door.
That very familiar voice changed his mood. Again his heart beat rate changed from normal to very fast and strong, like it used to in eighth grade.
Realizing that he was still in his lab coat, "Give me a minute." he said and turned back to the lab door to take off the coat. He hanged it back over Mr. T's and turned back again to the front door. To Hannah the lab coats would just appear as normal coats, but would definitely appear different if she saw Patrick in one of them.
He pulled open the door and tried to avoid making eye contact, but the blue sweater she had worn made the color of her eyes and uniqueness to come out real good. It made it that hard for Patrick to avoid them. He raised his eyes and got caught up in analyzing their every detail.
It was then Hannah who shied away her eyes and asked without even greeting "How far are you with your math assignment?"

"Oh that! I haven't started." He responded, and still gazed that awkwardly into her face.
"What!" She was shocked "This close to the submission date, and you haven't started?" she asked.
"Let's just say I work best under pressure."He invited her in and closed the door behind her, "I'll probably start on the last night before submission." He said. It being a little dim in the house he drew the blinds in the kitchen and the TV room to shine the late morning light into the house. He wouldn't have to turn the lights ON. "I figure you're here because you want us to do it together, right?" He asked passing to his room.

"Yep!" Hannah answered, "There are questions I find hard to understand and thought that since you're good in math you can shine a bit of light on them." she had to raise her voice a bit, to make sure Patrick heard her all the way from his room, "Maths is really not my thing, you know!"
Hannah had already done parts of the assignment with her friends during their afterschool study group meeting, but wasn't sure of the solutions she had, after all it was Veronica who came up with most of the solutions. She wanted to redo the whole paper with Patrick. She knew that with his help, she stood a better chance of getting over that seventy percent mark she set for herself...

The assignment that has been giving her study group a hard time for the past days was all of the sudden as simple as basic maths. Patrick had that ability, to break down one complex math problem into its simplest basic forms that even someone who was two grades away from it could understand it if they listened to him attentive enough.
They were on the last question of the assignment, when they heard a knock at the door.
"Wow, two visitors in one day!" said Patrick. For a person who doesn't get surprised easily, he was surprised.
He got to the door and opened it without asking who was behind it, he wanted to be surprised some more. But he wasn't when he realized that it was Hannah's younger sister, Portia.
She asked of her big sister, and Patrick immediately let her get through the door. She was setting foot for the first time inside that house.

After the message was received, Hannah followed after her little sister and told Patrick that she'll be back in a bit.
An hour passed without a sign of her return.
Patrick who at first waited patiently started doing the last question on his own, and finished it without Hannah ever returning.
She came over later that evening, and only to collect her things since Patrick had already done the last question on his own. She would just have to copy it into her answer sheet, but she didn't. She nicely asked him to explain how he solved it, saying there was no use having right answers she didn't understand. It only took twenty more minutes.
After Patrick walked her out, he made sure to lock the gate - something he wished he had done last night, because it was only then that she wouldn't have been able to enter through and ultimately depriving Patrick any lab work that day.

He came to enjoy his spaghetti meal in front of the TV with an animated movie on. He went to bed right after his meal, because he wanted to wake up early tomorrow and work on 'second theory' the whole of Sunday.

Sunday morning - he got up at approximately eight thirty in the morning. The sun was already up, and he could see the shimmering light through the closed blinds. It sure was a start of a perfect day to work on one of his two theories.
He did some fitness exercises in his room before heading for the bathroom. Habits he wanted to keep to everyday, but would sometimes go over two weeks without.
In the kitchen he made himself yet another big breakfast, enough to fill him for the next five hours or so. After cleaning up after himself, he went to put on proper clothing and came to stand in front of the lab door. He looked at the lab coats, but there was no smile on his face this time "Hypothesizing doesn't need a lab coat." He held onto the door handle and remembered what transpired yesterday when he was about to open the door, but he knew it was not going to happen again because yesterday after Hannah had left he made certain to lock the gate. There would be no visitor that day. But he was wrong. Because immediately when he unlocked the lab door, there at the front door sounded a hesitant silent knock.
He knew it was impossible for someone to be at the door. He listened for a few moments, hoping it would go away, but it did not.
He so much wanted to ignore it and enter the lab, but something unexplainable pulled him to the front door. It was like every step he took was not his own, that he was only watching. He could've sworn he was in a dream. He wanted to be angry, but he couldn't.
He unlocked the door, and slowly opened it. But immediately when he realized that it was his mother and father, both his parents, standing right there in the porch the shock woke him up, because he was in a dream.
He did not open his eyes. Even though he did not believe that he could re-enter the dream, he desperately tried it.
A minute passed, and he was still consciously awake. He clenched his fists and through his shut eyes silent tears burst.
By the time he opened his eyes, his pillow was heavy wet with salty tears. He threw the pillow on the floor and left the bedroom for the bathroom to take the longest shower he's ever taken.

Patrick entered the lab that Sunday at exactly ten thirty. On the board he wrote and erased, again and again he wrote and erased. Till finally he accepted that for 'second theory' experimentations he would not be transplanting only the brain but the whole head as a system from the neck up instead.
When he got out the lab it was around one PM, he decided that the rest of the day he would do his home-works while watching cartoons or skip both and play video games. Anything to help him stop thinking about the dream he woke from that morning.

He was done with his home-works when he realized that with 'theory two' experiments formulated; he would need experiment subjects soon.
A bottle of highly concentrated tranquilizer from the lab, he mixed it in with spaghetti meat balls. Whatever animal, no matter how big, if it ate the baited spaghetti that night he'd definitely find still unconscious in the morning. He defended his baiting skills as he spread the chunks of spaghetti on the lawn. And after all that was done he sat there on the edge of the porch and appreciated the starry skies above with the August evening breeze light on his cheeks...

Morning came and he woke up to the success of his set trap. Judging from the dog's size, it was about three months old if not a little younger. It would make a perfect first subject, to make all those mistakes on. He foresaw its gruesome future, a blood spattering death by a blade at his hands, and looked forward to it. How messed up was that?
Two more slices than usual into his lunch box. Busy placing the dog in the lab, he skipped his breakfast.
The moment he stepped outside the house to head to school he couldn't wait to get back, and start working on 'second theory' again just as he had done the previous day when he initiated it.
He walked much faster than he usually does. Thinking that the sooner he gets to school, the sooner the lessons will start. The sooner the lessons start, the sooner they will end. The sooner the lessons end, the sooner he'll get to come back home.
But his whole idea was wrong, he got to school five minutes before the first period, a period of which first fifteen minutes of were spent at the assembly which to him five minutes of felt like an hour.
The school principal had to address the whole school. Soft talkers can talk for long, and the principal of Roseville High, Mr. Lebese, was the

softest of them all. But what the light skinned black man, maybe in possession of blood traces of white folks in his blood, lacked in verbal harshness! He made up for in the deliverance of corporal punishment. Everyone feared going up to his office and pupils doing their final year had to also be wary of being late in the morning even by a single minute. And regardless his methods of discipline, no one really hated him except those who hated the idea of schooling itself. Every school has its own fair share of those, and more in some schools than others.

"Hello, Patrick." She greeted first. His eyes easy; he greeted back before gluing them on the board ahead and began fiddling unintentionally with his wrist watch again. He definitely had something more to say and she could tell. "Something on your mind?" she asked, she couldn't resist her own need to know what could have been bugging him so early on a Monday morning, not that he's ever that much different on other mornings.
He turned to her, looked her directly in the eyes "It's 'Friday'." He said evenly, "I can't get it out of my head. The more I try not to think about it, is the more I over think about it."
"I thought you would have forgotten by now." she said with a blush and tucked her face away from his heavy but gentle gaze, because she knew what he was talking and thinking about, "I was just talking in the heat of the moment, Patrick." She added and only because she felt the great need to explain herself to him.
"But it was not a bad idea." His voice pulled up her face, "I'm going to learn one day, might as well start now, don't you think?" He inquired with hopes that she'd agree with him.
But before she could say, the first teacher to class entered. The lesson was long and took forever to end.
Halfway through the lesson he turned to her, "Hey." A whisper, but enough to grab her attention, and when he gazed that long into her pretty eyes without saying a word, she smiled, "I wanna talk about Friday." He said lowly.
"Can't it wait till after school?" she asked yet hoped he'd talk about it right then either way. She's never gotten him that interested to talk to her before, and she has tried!
"It won't take long, I promise." He reassured still looking that steadily yet so lightly into her eyes.
"Okay." she said "Let's talk about Friday."
"I wanna learn, and I want it to be from you, Hannah." when he paused

to ask she smiled and blushed radiantly, "So will you teach me?"
"I'd like to, Patrick." She answered positively, "But...you've already proven to be smarter than me, in fact smarter than everyone in twelfth grade, so I doubt there's anything you could learn from me." there she went again, leading to have the wrong idea of what the socially distant boy next to her was talking about.
"I don't mean school stuff and you know it, Hannah, I already know everything I need to know about that." He said lowly, and his voice soothing to her ears she neared her face towards him till it was that uneasily close to his, but he would not fear to add on, "I mean being in an actual relationship with someone, I wanna experience that, you think you can help me?"
When she looked that intensely into his dusty brown eyes and at that close range, she knew, that he spoke from his mind at the least, from his heart at the most. How could she not kiss him right then, and satisfy her secret fantasies that fill her nights with confusions. How could she feel like that about another, while she has another to call her own?

"But you have to promise to listen, and most of all open up to me." she spoke silently yet audibly while looking into his eyes still, "You think you can do that, Patrick?" she held out her pinky. Ignoring the pinky he neared his face even closer to hers. She swore in that split of a second that he'd surely kiss her, but when he whispered '*the teacher is watching us*', she thanked that he didn't. Yet wondered what it would have felt like...
Patrick did not realize it, but he had totally forgotten about what awaited him back at the house, the dog. And as soon as he did, time seemed to slow down again. Even the last fifteen minutes of the last lesson of the day felt to drag for hours to him...

Patrick slowly opened the titanium door, but only to be greeted by a barrage of loud barks. He tried shushing it, but only made things worse. It's only a dog, he reminded himself, you feed it and it's ought to like you more than its absent owner or master.
When he walked out the lab twenty minutes later he and the dog were practically friends.

At the realization of dusk he jumped off the couch abruptly, last night's skies woke the wannabe astronomer in him. He wanted to watch the skies as the stars began to appear that night.
The aftermath of the sunset was still clearly visible when Patrick

spread the towel on the mowed grass - the redness in the horizon - it was beautiful nature.

But before he'd go down to lay on his back and get lost in analyzing the starry skies above, there she was! The only woman he'd learn and know to love in another's arms. Had he known of their shared future he'd hate seeing her with anyone but instead the whole scenery bugged his interest, he'd wonder what they were thinking in that moment right then in each other's arms like that. What were their thoughts, their intentions and to what end result did they do what they did to or rather with one another. And finally he'd ask himself what was love if not the chemical imbalance that forced and pushed animals towards mating. Mother nature's own trickery, and ace up her sleeve to ensure reproduction and continuation of species, love!

Hannah was a meter away from her home's gate when she turned her head to look at the boy who continued to walk up the street, and never bothered to take a moment to turn to look at her one more time. Whatever it was she was feeling for him, it was real, but mutual? That could be argued given the boy's history with young ladies.

After she got through the gate Patrick stopped observing and quickly remembered what he had initially come out to do - observing the stars as they began to appear. But it was too late for that. The stars already filled the skies above...

Like every other day, Patrick would pass the time in class drawing in his drawing book. And Hannah beside him would stare into the drawing trying to figure out what it was he was drawing this time. "I'm bored!" she began, "Let's do something fun, like play a fun game or something." She insisted already pulling Patrick's chair close to hers. But he resisted, planting his feet and pushed his weight down.

"If you're bored read your notes, or practice Math." His voice thick and snarly he added "We both know you need to improve that."

"Ouch! What side of the bed did you wake up on this morning?" she asked and neared him, curious to know what was wrong, but nothing was, according to him at the least.

"'What side of the bed did I wake up on'?" he echoed, "What does that even have to do with anything?" and before she could amusedly respond he added "Don't even answer that." He said, "Go to your friends or something, just leave me be for now." Something was definitely wrong with him, she was convinced.

Wanting to be a better 'friend' or whatever it was they were, she remembered how a gentle touch on her shoulder from that special person would always make her feel better, whenever she was having one of 'those' days. Coincidently that one special person to her was Patrick's mother. How could she still have not figured it out yet, the full extent of the identity of the boy she sat a mere hand's reach away from in class. And maybe if she would she'd be able to keep that long made promise to a dead woman, 'being a friend to her antisocial son.' But in a way she was already becoming that.
That close to Patrick she reached for his shoulder for that gentle therapeutic human touch. But immediately when she touched him 'suppressed' memories of his dead mother rushed into his head like a flashback. In his thoughts he could hear, feel, see, and even smell the presence of his mother as he slowly let the memories roam his imagination. For the second time since the death of his mother, he was walking down memory lane. The first time was when he replayed his thirteenth birthday in his head repeatedly trying to force his brain to dream of his parents during that night's sleep. But even then the picture of his mother wasn't that clear in his head and it had slowly been fading since. An automated coping mechanism, maybe. Patrick Mot has been struggling to hold on to any playback of the memories of his own mother. Yet just then when she held on to him, funny enough the same way his own mother would when she talked to him about a reported bad behavior at school. Everything came back to him. All the memories of his mother filled his head, and he could see the distinct features of her face like she was just standing in front of him so clear that he could have sworn to have the ability to draw her face from memory alone.

Overwhelmed by the memories; shock showed on his face, yet he smiled, and when she noticed his reaction to her touch, she let go. Still with the face of his mother in his head he turned his eyes and looked easily into hers, then a lonely tear from his right eye that he quickly wiped a little too late for she had seen it. She was confused, yet did not ask him to explain his reaction to her touch. She just looked back into his eyes. Her smile complemented Patrick's. They were having a 'moment', one you mostly see in movies or read of in romantic novels.
But being his-self the moment would not last, he frowned to her face and turned again to face his front.

"Can I ask you something?" She asked, already missing those dusted eyes, and patiently searched for them. But being herself too she did not wait for him to reply, "Why do you always do that?" she asked in real concern over the boy, "It would look like you're really happy, but as soon as you realize that someone else notices it, you turn cold to make them believe otherwise." She paused to ask again, "Why do you feel this need to keep up this sad lonely look?"
He turned his head to again look into her eyes, and the look in his eyes she would not soon forget, nor will she the words he said to her.
His slightly pinched cold gaze pierced that hard into hers. He spoke slowly, not even showing his teeth. "You have got this idea that you know me, the person that I am, you're wrong. Hannah you don't know me." He paused and minded his next words, "It will benefit you more than it does me if you stopped acting like you do." And he could see in her eyes the words crushing her down, "And you can go, if you no longer want to sit next to me, I'll understand." She was silent for seconds. But finally when she raised her eyebrows to him to let out words, Patrick stood up, and left the class without giving her the chance to speak.
Patrick finally had that answer to the question of why he has been struggling to remember the face of his mother. It's nice to have good memories of the dead, but it's a temporal fix that last only a few moments, and the moment it leaves all that remain is the hurt that comes with the realization of what you have lost. He wished he could forget again her face for she was all he saw when he closed his eyes.

It was not long before he returned to class with his hands dipped into his pockets, and his eyes glued to the floor dreading every moment he had to blink them.
Immediately when he sat down she turned and began at him, "You may be right, you know?" she said, "I may not know you as much as I think I do. But whose fault would that be? Mr. 'I rather not say', all you do when I talk to you is nod, shake your head, or say 'I don't wanna talk about it'." there was absolute truth in her words, and she wouldn't stop, because she knew that Patrick was listening and this he had hear if he hoped to be a better person in future. "You never really tell me anything I don't already know, you leave me guessing, and I doubt you even correct me when I'm wrong." she continued with the pitch of her voice changing as she got emotional, "So yes, you're right, I don't really know you, Patrick. But I want to, I really do. And meeting me halfway is

the least you can do - should do, don't you think?"
"I'm sorry." He said. And that's all he said back before folding his hands on the desk and tucking his head in.
But the young lady beside him wouldn't let him sulk away. She placed her hand on his back "Apology accepted." She said, and immediately Patrick sat back upright in shock, it was not from hearing that his apology was accepted. But like a while ago, when she placed her hand on him; vivid memories of his mother were triggered yet again.
"What's wrong?" she asked, "You did the same thing a while ago when I touched you. You don't want me to touch you, do you?" she asked.
And he'd quickly answer "No, I want you to touch me." she smiled when she heard how sexual it sounded, even though Patrick did not mean it that way. "I'm not used to being touched." he explained, "Let alone by a girl." He said.
"Well, you better get used to it Mr." she said, and the two began talking about the upcoming preparatory examinations.
But Patrick in his head could not stop wondering how her touch could have triggered the suppressed memories of his mother.
Their small conversation led them to talking about what they do when they are at their homes, and everything he told her was the truth. But he made sure not to talk about his lab works, just yet - Hannah didn't even know that the house had a laboratory. He kept that information from her because he still believed the time to let her in on the infinite project was not right, just yet...

Out on the grass Patrick playfully ran with the dog barking and chasing after him. Actual fun, he was capable of it.
Hannah walked out her house and headed straight for her gate. She was going to pass without saying anything but when he noticed her he ran in her direction and the dog followed, she too approached the fence. When they were a talking distance away but still with the fence between them she started surprised, "You have a dog?"
"Who doesn't these days?" He answered with a question that went unanswered.
"How come I've never seen it around?" She asked.
"Well I keep him locked up inside one of the rooms in the house...I only fear the worst to leave him roam the yard in my absence." He replied.
Again she asked "oh! Him! What's his name?"
"Oh SNERT! I never thought of that. Oh...that would work." He thought to himself and quickly responded "Snert! Snert is his name."

She looked at the dog and started calling to it "Snert! Oh Snert...Come here boy." The dog would not respond, it kept getting through Patrick's legs all the while trying to tear the bottom parts of his trousers, it was a playful dog, but all puppies are.
"I taught him better, he won't respond to voices he does not know." He said and turned his attention to the dog, but the dog was actually not responding because 'Snert' was not its name, but would have to be since Patrick said so.
"Oh! I see, that's really nice." She said, "Hey I've got to go, see you boys around." She walked away.
When he raised his eyes to find her, he saw her approaching him - the boyfriend. And envy swooped in yet again, but the dog gave needed distraction. He would not even notice when they kissed.
When the sun had touched down. Snert willingly followed after him back into the house. Exhausted he passed out on the couch and would only wake up the next morning for school...

CHAPTER FIVE: Embrace

From his sleep a nightmare yanked him out. Chances are if it was not for the nightmare he was going to oversleep, maybe even way past his school time. Curled still in the couch he raised in great effort to his eyes his wrist watch, but he could not see the digits. It would take a dozen more seconds for his eyes to adjust, but he had to keep them open. His palms pressed back together between his warm thighs he relaxed his eyes and passed that quickly back to sleep.
A few moments into his new dream with potential to turn into a wet one, he began to hear the faint rings of the alarm clock emanating from the bedroom.
In a hoarse voice he complained "No...It's got to be kidding me..." and plugged both his ears tightly with his hands.
For school he had to start preparing then if he did not want to be late and lose that chance to walk with her to school. The thought of losing a chance to walk with her motivated him to do the opposite of what his body was telling him to do. He rolled his body from the couch and literally fell to the near floor below, but used his hands to reduce the impact of the fall on his already beaten body.
A cold shower rather than a warm bath was ought to do it, he thought as he remembered how in the past his parents would praise the therapeutic effects of cold water in the morning.
The water from yesterday in the geyser was still warm, he decided that he would scrub with warm water and rinse off the foam with cold water.

It worked, as he felt ready to take on the day as soon as he walked out the shower.
But regardless his hurried preparation, he still left late for school and lost that day's chance to walk with her.
A lot has been on his mind lately. Including his prison visit that was way overdue. He hasn't seen the old man in over two months. And Alfred wasn't the person to call the house that often...

First thing first, he raised his eyes as soon as he got through the door to find the person sitting behind the desk that was beside his.
Before sitting down he greeted, "Hey you." His voice a little thicker

than usual, "How are you today?" He asked pulling his chair to sit down.
"I'm good and you seem good too, but your voice…" She paused as trying to recall something, "Wait I recognize that voice, it's the one you used back then when we did the math assignment together, I don't like it." She said, "It's a lil' scary."
"You should have said something." He paused to clear his throat, "How about now?" he asked "Do I sound any better?"
She smiled blushingly, affirmed with a nod and shifted her eyes back to her books, but she couldn't concentrate anymore no matter how hard she tried. The same as last night when she couldn't keep the boy next to her out of her thoughts that she conceded to her secret erotic desires and drifted willingly into her fantasies, thus failing to complete or do her school work.

Mid lesson, out of nowhere he turned to her "Do you ever think about me when you're home?" she froze and he neared in. "Because I do, and a lot, I always imagine how it would feel like to have a girlfriend, how it would feel like to have you as my girlfriend. Hey, would I be asking a lot if I asked you to play boyfriend and girlfriend with me, just for a while? To feel how it feels like?" He asked and again quickly thought *"Oh boy! Did I just ask her that? I hope I just thought that in my head."* From how she looked at him he could tell, that she heard him loud and clear and was thinking of a suitable response.
"You'll not be asking a lot, actually." She answered, "But it will be pointless, if we pretend to be boyfriend and girlfriend as you say, the feelings won't be real…" She explained.
"Fair enough, forget that I even asked…it was stupid of me." He said with his eyes turned to the board and quickly back to her, "Hey! Your cheeks are red, are you okay." he asked and instinctively placed the back of his fingers on her forehead, she laughed and everyone turned to stare. They found her in smiles!
Mrs. Ramsey watched and smiled too. Their Life Sciences teacher, was one of the teachers who suspected or rather insinuated that the two were attracted to one another and knew very well that trying to separate them was only going to pull them much harder towards each other. And like most teachers she hoped and wished that the young man's intellect would rub off on Hannah and help her get her grades higher…
"Now that we've covered most of this topic there'll be a term test on

Friday that will contribute to your term total mark." Said the teacher and that's all Patrick heard from that Life Sciences' lesson, he barely listened to any teacher, yet he was the top scorer on any and every test in that class in that school for that matter.
"Hey, Patrick, would it be okay if I came to your place to revise with you?" she asked, "All my study mates live too far from me and I've got chores at home every day."
"You don't have to explain." Began Patrick, "Just let me know what time to expect you."
"Say any time before sunset till we write the test." She said and went on to add "I need these marks, so I think if you helped me for two hours every day, I'll pass the test. Is that okay?"
"No problem at all." He said, "It gets lonely in the house, I could use the company."

Weekdays passed fast, and Patrick continued to grow fonder of the four legged friend. But deep down it was all pretence to him.
In the last three school nights Hannah had walked over to Mr. T's house to prepare for the upcoming Life Sciences' test. A test he would have still aced without revision.
Friday afternoon. Finally! The experiment that promised so much to Patrick was that close to being conducted. But would what the teenager theorized still seem attainable after the experiment?
He looked at the two lab coats hanging by the lab door and took a few deep breaths and thought 'here goes everything' before grabbing and putting on one that was his...

Three hours later Patrick opened the lab door and walked out with his lab coat more red than white with blood, the dog's blood. In the three hours the young self made scientist had learnt all he needed to know regarding the first part in his three parted second theory of the infinite project, decapitation. And taking in a gruesome manner the life of a small dog that was not even his own was a small but in his eyes a worthy price to pay. "I need a grave." He thought, before heading to the garage for a shovel and a pick.
He buried the dog right in the middle of the lawn and hoped grass would grow there to cover the ugly patch of dirt.

Just minutes after he had gotten back into the house through the back door, he heard knocks at the door. Part of him had a pretty good idea of who it was, "I'll be there in a minute." He said out loud turning OFF the

TV that had turned itself ON when the cartoons started at five as he had set it to. He then quickly rushed to his room to take off his muddy shoes and rushed back out barefooted, *"What could she possibly want today?"* He thought.

Hannah had just taken a bath and her skin looked more radiant than ever, there was no way he was not going to notice it with his observant eye.
When he opened the door and gazed at the beauty that stood in front of him, he froze in awe. When Hannah greeted him all he could say back was 'Wow!' silently to himself, but Hannah could make the word that remained glued on his lips.
The white page she handed him unfroze him, "You left in a hurry and left this." She said, and tried that hard to think about anything else other than how Patrick looked at her, the way every girl wants to be looked at.
"It's about school, tomorrow!" She said when she noticed that he wasn't even interested in reading it, "Read it, okay? I'll see you tomorrow, at school, Patrick!" Stressed Hannah almost as if she knew that Patrick intended not to go to school tomorrow, it was a Saturday after all, and maybe the monitor had told her of Patrick's intentions to not attend the extra classes.
"Yeah...yeah...I'll do all that." Patrick replied.
When Hannah turned to walk to the gate, Patrick thought that he should walk her out. He came to walk that close beside her.

"I saw you digging over there, were you planting a tree?" She searched for his eyes like she always does, "It would be beautiful to be right in the middle of the grass like that."
"No, I was burying Snert." replied Patrick, why wouldn't he lie? "He died." he said, and there it was, the lie! The dog did not just die, he killed it, and not by accident.
"When?" she asked shocked, "What happened? I saw how you played with it, you must have loved it. Are you okay though?" she was sorry for him, but wouldn't be so if she knew the truth. She would be disgusted at the least.

Patrick did not answer any of her questions, "I will never forget the good time I had with him, especially our last hours together." He said meaning the experiment, those were the moments he cherished most with the dog. "He was more than just a dog to me." He added. His

words were true. Snert was the light at the end of the tunnel. After the experiment the procedure seemed more practical than before. The brutal murder of the dog was not in vein.
"That's sad...you look like you need a hug." She replied as she walked even slower, and much closer to Patrick, that their shoulders brushed. In her own way, she was offering to give him a hug, but Patrick was caught up in playing hurt that he did not even realize it. The two made it to the gate and only Hannah went through. When she turned to say bye, she found him standing equally between the open gap of the gate arms high stretched and reaching for the overhead metal crossbar. As he hung there his shirt lifted leaving him bare from the waist line to no more than five centimeters above the belly button. But that alone was enough skin, enough to incite her young adult sensual desires. She took two steps towards him, with no clear intents of what to do next, but she did want to do something because she did not want to leave, right then retiring to her house was the last thing on her mind.
Like a goofy adrenalin junky Patrick attempted to lift his feet off the ground to see how long he can hold his weight but his grasp gave way and when he missed his landing he stumbled forward, almost bumped into her.
His hands grabbing instinctively for balance onto her waists he spoke softly with relief, his mouth so close to hers that she could feel the current of air blown out his lips as he spoke. "That was close." He said and looked erotically into her eyes, uncharted as those territories were to him it seemed as if he knew what he was doing. But he did not. This was one field he was inexperienced in.

Weakened at her knees by his gaze and nearness, she shied her face to look at the ground below them. But she did so only to search for the courage to do something she has been waiting too long for him to do first, kiss. When she slowly raised her head to definitely kiss him she was met with the infamous frown, and she would not kiss him, yet.
His hands still attached to her waists she held on to his forearms and pressed gently with her fingers, it gave him goosebumps.
Looking deeply into his eyes she had to ask "What's wrong?" her breathing was different. "What did I do?"
"Your boyfriend." He said briefly without a flinch.
"Don't worry about him." she replied, "I'll end it with him. I've always wanted to, and now I have a reason to." she meant it.
"Why would you do that?" he asked and slowly his frown faded.

"It's you." She answered sure of herself, "I wanna be with you, Patrick Mot." She said it finally. There was no going back now.

There was a pause in his response, and it felt like forever to her. But eventually he spoke "I don't deserve you." If he knew his response did her more harm than justice he would have not said it, "Hannah, I'm not the person I've made you to believe me to be. And when I said 'your boyfriend', what I meant was that he's looking at us, and now he's heading towards us."
She had been caught, yet she would not scare. She turned to confirm and it was true, Kgomotso had been watching them since the moment Hannah walked through that gate witnessing their little moment.

She turned back to Patrick, "Please go." She said evenly, "And lock the gate, I'll deal with him."
From her hips Patrick raised his right hand to her shoulder and traced the tips of his fingers down her arm still looking that seductively into her beautiful eyes. How could she still want to kiss him with her boyfriend right there? She wondered. But it was easy really, she loved him, and has for a very long time, longer than she realized.
"See you tomorrow at school." he said and would not walk away without his last say. Minding the shortening distance of the approaching boyfriend he made sure to lower his voice and looked steadily into her eyes to say "I wanna be with you too, but I have to tell you everything first. I'll be thinking about you tonight." He ended and turned inside after exchanging a rival stare with Kgomotso who seemed rather less infuriated...

When he woke up in the morning, it was of the sound of the alarm clock. The loud rings had cut short his dream, and once again Hannah was in it.
By then he was aware of the effect she had on him. Though he could not put it in words to explain, he was aware of everything that was happening between them and knew for certain that the attraction was mutual, she had made that clear last evening.

For time was on his side he prepared for school like any other day without any rush.
By quarter of an hour before eight Patrick had finished preparing for school and was then patiently waiting for Hannah. Yesterday before their 'moment' she had told him that as soon as she had completed

getting ready for school she'd come get him. Patrick wasn't a fan of going to school on Saturdays or attending any form of extra classes. He saw no point in it; his grades were exactly where he wanted them to be.
But Hannah wouldn't be able to come through to get him, on command last evening fearing Kgomotso's outburst of anger she had told Patrick to lock the gate. Remembering that, Patrick rushed out to go unlock the gate, he found her already at it. They walked together back to the house, quiet, both awaiting the other to bring up the events of the previous evening, but neither would...

That afternoon back at the house Patrick paced around the kitchen making a list of things he would have to buy tomorrow in town. When he got into the lab he caught sight of the tranquilizing mixture from yesterday's experiment - he would use the same mixture to catch another dog or this time a cat, for his next experiment...

The sun was already high and burning hot by the time Patrick was ready to leave for town that Sunday. But he never bothered to put on a hat. He'd have to bear the late Sunday morning sun's heat to the nearest cab hotspot...

He spent only thirty minutes inside the prison. And that would be his last visit. For the first time in over four years the old man had good news to relay to Patrick. But it was not the length of his sentence. That had not changed. Alfred would still serve his full sentence. It was how he was going to serve the other half of it that had changed. Alfred was going home. In that December when his served time reaches exactly five years, its halfway mark, he'd be released into house arrest where he'd remain till he finishes his one decade sentence. Patrick would not be alone anymore in the house.

After paying the house bills at the bank he headed for the towns mall for his groceries.
First thing on his shopping list was unsurprisingly spaghetti and when he got into the first shop packs of spaghetti were the first items he loaded on the shopping trolley. He also bought bathroom supplies, and had actually forgotten to put them on the list. And one thing he made sure not to forget was the chocolate bar - his new plan relied on it. When Hannah saw him leave for town, she asked him to buy her a chocolate bar. But when he returned home he'd not find her waiting for

him at the gate just as she said she would.
He had bought her one of the biggest there were in the shop where he bought it, and surprisingly his only motive was that she would have enough that she won't ask for it again if ever there is a next time that she will see him going to town again. But that was one wrong analysis he could ever have, buying her the biggest slab is most likely the reason she'd ask him for another if there's ever a next time.

Halfway through a movie there it was, the knock at the door. He knew exactly who it had to be.
On his way to the door he went to take the chocolate bar from the refrigerator. He had kept it in there just so it would not melt. He wanted it to retain its appealing shape. "Here goes everything." He said silently to himself, it was time to put his plan in motion.
When he opened the door and found her behind it looking more beautiful than ever, he just handed her the bar of chocolate and without raising his eyes to her still, he said "There you go, one non-white chocolate bar for you." Hannah had made it clear that white chocolate was not for her.

Seeing that Patrick did not intend on inviting her in and was in an odd mood she began anyway "Thanks a bunch." And quickly added still trying to find his eyes "Hey, you're different today."
Patrick raised his eyes to meet hers and made no attempt whatsoever to hide the scowl on his face "No, I have always been like this, it's just that today you happened to notice." He was looking that steadily back into her eyes "My movie is ending, you should go enjoy your chocolate and I should go finish my movie, see you tomorrow, Hannah." He said and slowly closed the door with her standing in front of it.
He stood behind the door till he heard the drag sound of the closing gate "It's only for the best." He said.
Alienation! Patrick enjoyed the company of a friendly face, but he knew it was only a matter of a short time before Hannah would be way more than just a friendly face to him, not that is a bad thing to have someone you love. But his reasoning sought of made it a bad thing for him. He had to choose, he was going to have to choose either way, between the infinite project and her since they'd both require his time and attention. And obvious truth and fact was that he could not do both, he had to choose.
He could choose to give in to love at the hope of growing old with that one special person who's hand you'd want to hold on to and their voice

be the last you hear when they or take your final breath on this earth with one thought in mind 'I have lived and loved, I have no regrets!' and pass out into the unknown. Or he could choose to submit his self to solitude and work tirelessly in his mentor's laboratory in desperate hope of curing his own mortality to make himself live forever. But should he fail he'd most probably die alone with one thought in mind 'I have not lived nor loved, if only I could go back in time.' as he passed away from this earth. But there is also a catch in choosing love. The person you vow to live for and grow old with could die a little too early plunge you into a life of misery for the rest of your days. And his last months with his own father were an indisputable proof of that...

Monday morning, Patrick woke up still with the idea of alienation fresh in his head.
Out the yard to walk down the road to school, part of him did hope to see her on the road. He did try to ignore these hopes, but there was no use as he saw her come out the house almost as if she had been waiting for him to walk out the house. He did not wait to hear her call out to him before he could stop, he did so on his own.
Yet again she struggled with the old gate, Patrick approached in silence to aid her, he would not speak. Even when she greeted he only nodded back with his lips sealed still.
The walk was silent, at first, for it was not long before she asked "Why are you like this?"
"Like what?" the vibrations in his voice carried the scent of anger.
"I mean serious all of the sudden." She said "And not just serious, rude too. Why?" she added and even he could tell how much it was breaking her, him being like that towards her. Nothing hurts more than a cold shoulder from someone you love. Yet Patrick would not stop, his choice was clear and he would stand by it no matter what, he self assured. He would chase immortality rather than seat back, relax and let himself fall in love.

In class he would almost make her cry with his rude responses and inconsiderate of her emotions. And had she been in different setting where no one would see her cry, she would have.
'Why?' - That was the one question she couldn't answer, why was he being like that, and she forced herself to ask him again and again she went unanswered every time...

Two more dogs, pups, his trap was good. And they two he had to gain their trust like the first lab dog that was no more, Snert, who was brutally killed and the murder justified in his head as the typical result of any first science experiment.
To the puppies he was the actual monster to be feared, but as soon as he brought food into the lab he was their savior, only in their eyes of course and everyone who would see him with them not knowing his plan for them both. But even hatchlings do open wide their mouths to their predators.

Once he was done sweeping the house he checked his wrist watch and calculated that he can make it to the pet shop and be back in time for his five O'clock cartoons if he tock his bike. He had to buy the pups dog foods. And if he hurried he'd have enough time to play with them in the lawn first, before coming to watch his animated TV series.
Back from the pet store, and already barefooted on the grass with the dogs out of the cage the running began. The dogs chased and he tried his best not to run too fast or too slow.
He tired first, he went on all fours and that only riled them up more. They would not let him catch his breath. He was having fun, the puppies too.
While kneeling down, the gate slid open. He raised his head to take sight of the unscheduled visitor.
He was surprise to see that it was Hannah.

Finding him in smiles she greeted first, but for the first time she was hesitant not knowing how he'd respond, "Hey Patrick.", and part of her did not want to know.
"Hi…" Patrick greeted back and Hannah from his different voice tone could tell that Patrick was different again from how he had been in the past couple of days. It gave her relief in regard to the subject that had brought her there.
"So what brings you here?" he asked glancing at the side bag Hannah carried with her.
"We have the math test on Friday…Sir Peterson said that we should practice in pairs, remember?" She answered, "So I chose you for a partner."
"And you didn't tell me that in class…why?" Patrick asked, he stood up and started snapping his fingers to rile the puppies up. Again trying his best not to make eye contact with her, usual Patrick.
"Well with your mood lately I knew you were going to refuse if I asked

you then." She explained and simultaneously caught the smile that Patrick gave the dogs and continued "So I thought I'd just show up, I don't really think you're that cold to chase me away right now, or are you?" She dared him, a risk, but a calculated one.
"Well you know the way, I'll find you inside." He said.
But she could not resist asking first, "So who are these?"
"I've only named the male, his name is 'Snert Junior.' I'm still thinking on a name for the female." He answered briefly and ran towards the cage and the puppies ran after him, he got them both through the hatches and followed Hannah into the house with the cage in hands.
When he stopped to open the lab door Hannah stopped too, "Why does this room have such a strange door?" she asked "I've always wondered what you keep in there."
"Still curious I see." He thought before answering, "This is my evil lair." When Hannah asked what was an evil lair he replied to say "That's for me to know and for you to wonder, go to the TV room already…I don't want you to see what's behind this door, not yet anyway." He purposely said so to make her even more interested to know what's behind that strange door. With her he knew exactly which buttons to push.
When Patrick got out the lab he told Hannah that he had to watch his cartoons first before doing any math. Hannah agreed and told him that she had asked her aunt to study till seven with him and that she had agreed…

With how talkative Patrick got through the revision Hannah concluded that the anger Patrick had been carrying around in the past couple of days was just grief over the death of his dog. She even asked to confirm her own conclusions "So Patrick is that it? You've been acting up for the past two days because you lost your dog? And now you're over it because you got replacements?"
"I'm not saying that…you are." He said and then added with an apology sincere enough "I just want to say I'm sorry for treating you like I did in the past two days, how can I make it up to you?" and that was it! Once again he discarded an idea due to emotions he did not comprehend. First he halted 'first theory' now he was discarding alienation, two ideas that both had a speeding effect on his ultimate project, cheating death and staying superior to it.
Hannah refused the offer with an explanation "Nah it's fine, I understand, plus I would've reacted the same if not worse if it was I

who lost something dear to myself."
After Patrick had told her to suit herself for refusing the offer, the two of them continued to study mathematics, but it was not all both of them thought of, they secretly thought of each other, and frequently at it.
Whenever Patrick would explain a solution that proofed hard for her to get on her own, he would get lost in her eyes and she'd have to call him back to earth. She was by then used to him just tuning out on reality and escaping elsewhere from time to time like that. She did always wonder where was his mind really going and whenever she asked, she knew that the responses he gave her were false, that made her wonder even more.

After forty five minutes through the revision Patrick asked that a short break be taken and she agreed. He had to feed the puppies, he told her and also told her to help herself to anything to drink in the fridge, it be juice or water, whatever she preferred.
She found the juice in the refrigerator of course, but did not know where to look for glasses. She called out to Patrick who had already entered the lab. Not knowing that the lab was sound proof she kept calling and all her calls went unanswered.
She'd have to find the glasses on her own. And it was only a matter of time before she opened the right cupboard, and she did and took out one of the large sparkly glasses. She rinsed it with water from the sink tap before pouring herself fruit juice in it.

When he walked out the lab her glass was still full, she must have liked the juice so much that she poured herself a second glass full, he thought.
She immediately asked when Patrick knelt back down "Were you ignoring me again, like you do in class?"
Not knowing what she was talking about he simply said "No."
She asked again "You did not hear me call you several times while you were in that strange room?"
"Well I couldn't have heard you even if you screamed at the top of your lungs." He answered "You see the walls to that room are kind of sound proof."

Hannah began equally impressed as she was surprised "Firstly a strange door, secondly you don't want me to see what's behind the strange door and now the walls to the room with the strange door that

you don't want me seeing what's behind are sound proof." and asked intrigued with the mystery of the room "There really is something going on in that strange room...isn't there? And I bet it's something strange, isn't it?"
He turned to her and forced a sinister smile and said "Like I said before, you're not ready to know just yet." while looking straight into her eyes.
She said no word in return, she just pulled the books close to her and the two continued with their math revision.
Patrick couldn't help it but take a peek into her eyes whenever he thought she wouldn't notice, but she was noticing. Just that she did not want to notice him that she was noticing him noticing her.
Even just to ask a simple math related question he first had to practice it in his head. He actually wanted whatever he said to her to come out perfect, and he was aware of the fact that he was actually trying to impress her.
When they decided on a problem to solve individually and then present the answers to one another, he rushed to find a solution, again to impress her, which ultimately led him to make silly math mistakes that she corrected. A correction he hated, thought it made him appear less, the opposite of how he wanted to appear to her. Little did he know that it was actually bringing them even closer to one another than either could realize.

Seven O'clock approached and their revision had to pause till the next afternoon, but Patrick only became aware of the time when it was already minutes past seven. "Hey...look at the time...it's already thirteen minutes past seven." He said.
Hannah was shocked and had to confirm what Patrick was saying by pulling out her phone inside her side bag, it was a modern touch-screen smart phone. "She's going to kill me, I'm gonna be so dead." said Hannah referring to her aunt who had only agreed that Hannah could stay out till seven O'clock. She was only of course exaggerating about getting killed. She'll only shout at her. But that alone to a girl is enough to bring out streams of tears.

Patrick replied to say "Please don't be dead, I can't afford to lose another one." He was aware that she didn't mean getting 'killed' literally.
She quickly caught up to what he meant and asked "Wait, are you equating me to your dead dog?"

"Yes." He began "In a good way, of course. I just can't afford to lose someone I…Someone who I believe I'm beginning to...Someone I'm becoming friends with, who I feel I like being around and feel the same way about as I did Snert." He struggled to find his words yet didn't feel like stopping trying to explain to her what he meant.

Hannah even though knew exactly what Patrick meant she yet again asked "And how did you feel about Snert?"
In response he only said "Don't play dumb Hannah, you know what I mean."
"Yeah I know…I just want to hear you say it." She replied "Just to be sure."
Patrick turned his eyes to her to maybe confess his love to her, but found her face uncomfortably close to his and panicked.
He did what every panicked person in his shoes would have done at that moment - deviated from the subject. "Look at the time, you better get going." He said and after she affirmed he helped her get her books into her side bag and led her to the door which he made sure like a gentleman to open for her and let her go through first.

It was not that dark outside and the porch lights were ON, so were the street lampposts. He walked with her to the gate. They were walking really close to one another, so uncomfortable for Patrick that he couldn't even get his walking rhythm right.
When they got to the gate Patrick opened it for her to go through and he followed her out. They got to her home gate and he slid it open for her, but before she went through it, she turned to Patrick to do something he did not expect.
She turned to him, smiled and opened wide her arms to hug him - he hesitated at first before giving in. Immediately when their bodies touched he felt this new kind of warmth he's never felt before accompanied by the blood rush. Only if he knew where the blood was headed.
Heavily he held on tighter to her and whispered in her ear "I don't wanna let go, please don't let go." His voice, sad, she could sense the loneliness in it, yet he heard her laugh a bit, if he could see her face he would've seen how she blushed.

"But you have to." She whispered back, sweetly so. But deep inside wishing that he didn't have to, that time could stop and they'd stay in each other's arms like that forever without letting go.

His chest against her breasts, torso against torso, his heart raising against the passing of seconds and hers not falling far behind, the rapid thumps of their hearts intertwined like those of lusty lovers touching for the first time after being days apart from one another.
With their bodies pressed 'intimately' so, the most natural thing started to happen, Patrick was getting aroused.
He could feel his member tighten in his drawers under his trousers and got the sudden urge to urinate. *"Oh! Boy! What do I do now?"* He thought and panicked of the unknown climax he felt he was approaching, and fast.
It had been over one long minute into the hug when she started to loosen her grip over him, and so did he loosen his over her till their hands where by their sides, and her forehead resting on his chest just under his right collar bone.
He thought that she let go because she felt his member erect away from his body only to press hard against her. But she did so because of her own stimulated state. She was aroused as much as he was.
She pulled further out, really slow. When their bodies separated Patrick reached for her hands and held the four of her fingers excluding the thumbs in each of his hands.
She would ask searching smoothly for his eyes "Hey, why do you most of the times hide your eyes from me?"

Lowly he replied "I fear that you might see the truth in them, for the eyes can never lie, so I've heard my mother say." The light from the lamppost they stood close to was reflected in them.
"What truth?" She asked, but actually to confirm her thoughts of what was that truth that Patrick felt the need to hide from her.
"I think…"He paused and started again "I think...you should go, we don't want your aunt to kill you, do we?" Still looking at her with eyes of admiration, almost as if wanting to kiss her, maybe he did. Too bad he didn't know how to "It's gonna feel like forever till I see you again tomorrow."
She knew that's not what he meant to say, though the response did not disappoint her for she had a pretty good idea of what was the truth that he feared she might see in his eyes. "You have to let me go." She said again wishing that he wouldn't let go.
Patrick only let go of one set of fingers, her right set "But I don't want to let go." And that was exactly what she desperately wanted to hear coming out of his mouth.

"You have to or else I won't be alive tomorrow for you to hold on again?" She said smoothly still with the gaze into his eyes, but they lowered slowly to his lips and thoughts of kissing him once again invaded her mind, she only awaited the initiation from him, but she stood there beautifully disappointed.
"So are you saying we will do this again tomorrow?" He asked already loosening his hold for her to pull her fingers away, not that the hold was tight, it was the gentlest grasp she ever felt from a boy. Emotions with her and Kgomotso never got that intense, the thoughts Patrick evoked in her she never knew she was capable of thinking, the things he made her want to do to him, or rather with him.
"If you want to, yes." she answered and got through the gate in reverse for her hand was free from his hold then.
"*If what I feel for him is love then what am I feeling for this boy? What could be more than love?*" she thought evaluating her feelings for her boyfriend still with her thoughts for the inexperienced boy in any sort of relationship before her. "Good night, Patrick." She said.
"No! Great night, Hannah!" He corrected and helped her to lock the gate.

Wednesday morning - Patrick woke joyful, even better than how it used to be when he still lived with his folks.
He kicked himself off the bed with a hyperactive thrust and reached for the alarm clock to turn it off in advance, he had once again woken on his own before it could go off. But this time he would not complain.
Still in his room after the morning routine exercises he began to wonder if what he believed occurred last night had really happened or if it was just another one of his dreams where he gets so convinced that are reality till he wakes up from them, eventually.
When he found the books in the TV room on the table before the wide screen he couldn't help but smile all by himself. The books were confirmation that what he believed had happened last evening had really happened, that it was not a dream, Hannah was there!

School out Patrick had to help his Physical Sciences' teacher, Mr. Ossepea, Joel Ossepea, or Mr. Oss as the pupils of Roseville High called him, carry the demonstration apparatus for that day's experiment back to the school lab.
When the two got to the lab they found Sir Jackson still in it - the same teacher who taught Natural Sciences to Patrick in both eighth and ninth grade.

Sir Jackson quickly recognized Patrick and greeted "Afternoon, young man." He seemed rather happy to see him, he barely saw him since he didn't have a period in his class.
"Afternoon to you, sir." he greeted back putting the apparatus on top of one of the few counters that were in the school laboratory.
Sir Jackson then asked "So how's this lad doing in class? He was my top student back in both eighth and ninth grade, you know." and added sure of himself "A true born genius."

The bald headed and small eyed Mr. Oss turned to Patrick who was standing against the counter and began with a humorous smile to Sir Jackson's question of how Patrick was doing in his final year, "Well he's good, and I believe if he stopped playing in class he'll be great." Too bad both teachers didn't realize that Patrick was satisfied with being 'good' in class and had no interest in being anything more than that.

"And how's your father doing, Patrick? I haven't written to him in a while." Sir Jackson asked, of Mr. T of course, and not Mr. Mot who's the real father of the young man before them.
"He's doing pretty well actually. I went to see him this past Sunday." He answered and remembered to add "Oh! And he's also getting out this December. They are putting him under house arrest back at home."

"Wow that's great, can't wait to see him, I bet that place made him old, hasn't it?" Sir Jackson asked again, but he got another question before he got his answer from Patrick.
It was Mr. Oss who asked "So you know his father?"
Sir Jackson turned to him and began "Remember Alfred? Alfred M. Tobetsa? The one we went to varsity with...that's him, that's his father, small world right?"
Mr. Oss turned his eyes to Patrick again and said "Oh, T! I didn't know he had a son, but I can see the resemblance now, I guess brains can be inherited too." The impressed teacher continued "Son, your father was and still is a genius, you should aim to be greater than him, and believe you me...you have the potential to really surpass him and make him really proud. I know potential when I see one and you..." He intensified his voice to make sure Patrick got the message "You've got the talent son, it's just sad to see you settle for less when we all know, yourself included, that you're capable of so much more than settle for."
"What are the odds?" Sir Jackson began "I told him the very same thing when he was still my student as a freshman."

It was funny how everyone profiling Patrick deduced that he was settling for less than he was capable of. But the truth was that he was not settling for less at all. He was actually aiming way higher than any human ever should according to all religions and believes, let alone at his age or the age he began his quest.
I mean to ask; does it get any higher than what he was aiming for? It is every human's dream to die after reaching their life's goal or purpose, meaning whatever they aimed for or even ever dreamt of achieving in their wildest dreams was still beneath death. Death had control over whether they'd achieve that goal or not in their lives. But Patrick aimed to remove that uncertainty by gaining superiority over death itself. Again, it doesn't get any higher than that in life when aiming for a goal to achieve. Immortality is the ultimate goal which meant everyone was wrong about Patrick, except for Mr. T, of course. Patrick wanted the nectar, the fruit of the gods, which when consumed by mortals granted immortality and a chance at a seat beside the gods. He wanted to live forever, No dream can or goal can ever be bigger than that.
The two teachers began talking about their old days when they were still in varsity. Patrick knew that he had to show himself out or he'll never get to leave. He tiptoed out the lab without asking to be excused…

After feeding the pups he still had an hour before his five O'clock cartoons and Hannah hadn't arrived yet. Video games on his laptop seemed the best option to pass the time, plus he hadn't played them in a while, a long while. His last auto saves on F.E.A.R dated back to mid April.
Forty minutes into the game he heard the knock at the door, he knew exactly who it was yet he asked "Who is it?"
"It's me, Patrick." She answered back.

Patrick opened the door and behind it stood Hannah in a green sweater. The way she liked sweaters, she must have known that they looked good on her. "Do come in." Patrick invited her in.
When the two passed the lab door Hannah turned to it "One day I'll learn the secrets behind this door." She said before walking past. Patrick followed behind her and said "And it may come a lot sooner than you think."

Immediately when Hannah sat down on the couch she started after seeing what Patrick had been doing on the laptop "Really, Patrick, you

were playing video games? When you have a test on Friday and preparatory exams in no more than two weeks?"
He closed the lid of the laptop and replied "It was only today, plus I didn't want to start without you."
"No need to make excuses Patrick, let's begin." She said taking her books out of the side bag she carried them in, "We have so much to do today." She said.
"I still get to watch my cartoons, right?" he asked pulling the table nearer to Hannah who was already kneeling down. She seemed rather impatient.
"No, not today, Patrick." She refused him without even giving it a second thought, "Patrick, I really need to pass this test, I don't like my current grades and you're the only person who can help me." she added.
"Okay, whatever the lady wants." He said so not appearing to be concerned about missing his favorite cartoons. He had a backup plan for watching that afternoon's episode. He was going to watch the omnibus of the week's episodes on Saturday morning. And if he missed that too he can always download the episode from the internet.
He went to fetch his books from his room, and the two began their math revision for the upcoming test...

Like the afternoon before; Patrick asked that a break be taken after the first hour of the revision. And again like the previous afternoon he told Hannah that there's juice in the refrigerator if she wants some. He stood to go to the lab to feed the puppies and refill their water bowls yet again, he was fattening them, fattening them for their deaths.

He came out the lab sooner than he did the previous afternoon. He walked out with a page in hand "Look what I found." He said as he handed it to her and continued to say "Our break is left with only five minutes, you have that long to go through that."
"What is it?" She asked, "Oh! I see...first theory huh..." she said just after reading the title at the top of the page.
She read all that was on that page before she turned to Patrick "Wow! This is interesting, it's better than the other one in terms of brutality. So what are they exactly?" she asked interested to know more.

Patrick looked at her *"The sooner I tell her the better."* He thought to himself and said "Come by Saturday and I'll tell you all about it...who knows, maybe you might even get to see what's behind the strange

door." And changed the subject "Now let's get back to math, shall we?"
After the invitation and Hannah accepting it by telling him that she'll definitely come by on Saturday they got back to doing math. Patrick couldn't wait for the revision to end that evening so that he could get another hug from her, he really enjoyed the last, and the same could likely be said for Hannah. No wonder she seemed impatient during the revision.
He was again the one to tell her when the time to halt the revision till the next day was up, exactly at seven O'clock that time around.

Once her books were all back into her side bag she stood and Patrick led the walk to the door. Like a gentleman he still would not let her open the door herself. Awkwardly silent they walked slowly to the gate so close to one another that they could hear each other's breathing if they stopped to listen. So easy to tell what they both were thinking about or rather feeling right at that moment. The lusty anxious anticipation of what was to happen as soon as they walked through that gate.
Before they knew it, they were at the gate, he slid it open and they both got through.
But surprisingly Hannah would not act upon the desires of her heart as it seemed her intentions to walk through the next gate without even turning her face to the boy who followed like a lovesick puppy closely behind her. Yet she expected him to stop her, desperately wanted him to. She wanted him to enforce his masculinity upon her. She wanted him want her as much as she wanted him.
And like he could read her mind Patrick realizing that she was going to walk through the next gate without giving him the 'hug' he so longed for extended his hand and grabbed hers. He pulled her gently towards himself, and she did not resist. Because that was exactly what she wanted.
She walked right into his chest with open arms and a vivid smile. They wrapped their arms around one another for that affectionate embrace. Her body pressed against his body warmed him to the core that when she began to pull away he pulled her back into his demanding self and murmured softly into her ear "Please don't let go!" the second hug and he was already addicted to the soft and warm touch of her body, he craved more of her, and she would not deny him.

Snugly wrapped around his arms she tilted up her head a little, but enough that her soft lips were placed upon his bare neck. She could feel

the chills it gave him as she moved her lips up slowly against his neck with an erotic brush. And when she would place those lips heavily on his to pry them open the antisocial boy would still remain idle offering no response at all.
She pulled her face back a bit, their lips just inches apart, and opened her eyes slowly to look up into his.
Blushingly with her voice at the audible lowest and soft on her lips as it would be in his ears she asked "Why don't you kiss me back?"
"I don't know how to." He softly responded pleasantly shocked by the kiss but at the same time feeling a sense of satisfaction yet he wanted more of the feeling, craved it, lusted for it "I've never kissed anyone before." He said.

"Oh! I didn't know." she returned "But I'll still expect you to kiss me back tomorrow evening, I have to go." She ended with a smile like always, and turned to her gate.
Patrick remained there, watching as she walked towards the house. But before she'd open the front door she turned, and was surprised pleasantly to see him still standing there, watching her. She waved 'goodbye' and only then did Patrick turn to walk back to the house...

Later that night after the shower that left him shivering he went straight to bed. But he was too joyful to fall asleep without tosses and turns.
Thoughts started pouring into his mind and one that he could not ignore was that Kgomotso was most definitely not going to like what he's been doing as well as what he intended to do with her, the girlfriend, Kgomotso's girlfriend. She had not yet ended things with him just as she said she was going to the other day.
If a fight would ever break loose between the two, Patrick knew for certain that he'd lose. And spend the next few days plotting his perfect revenge. One he'd certainly deliver...

CHAPTER SIX: Love defining acts

"The truth is I still haven't decided yet, I don't even think about it much. What about you?" he asked in return, "What are your plans after high school, what will you do?" But Patrick already knew all she had to say back. He still remembered that first day of eighth grade when his classmates one by one were asked what they wanted to be when they grew up like it was just yesterday, which included Hannah's response of wanting to be a nurse when she grew up. Only if he knew who inspired her to be one. His mother!

Before they knew it, they were walking through the school gate. When they got to class with Patrick following that close behind Hannah after showing her through the door like a gentleman; one of their class mates - Veronica yet again - addressed the two of them as love birds, it was that obvious to their classmates, and had been way before the two even cared to think of its possibilities...

Time flew by and school out that fast. When Hannah stood to follow her friends to the door, Patrick held her by the straps that hanged from her back pack. He gently pulled her down to his desk. He looked up into her eyes and stated his desires, "I want to walk home with you." and looked away as soon as she got the message. Maintaining eye contact was still tricky for him.

"Are you coming or not?" Veronica already at the door called out to her friend "You can see him later at his house." She added and every boy in that class who heard her envied to be Patrick.
"Go on without me I'll catch you on the way." She responded to her and turned to Patrick "Then get your things already." She said.
"I need some water first, I'll be quick" Said Patrick and stood to exit the class.
Going to the taps was just a plan he devised so that when he and Hannah leave the class to head home, Hannah's friends would be so far ahead that they won't catch up to them. He wanted Hannah all to himself...

He made her laugh and she made him smile, in simplicity they made each other happy. They walked slower than everyone else on the streets, and soon it was only them left walking along the road. So slow yet they would realize it, deep in conversations that brought laughter and smiles, they very much enjoyed each other's company. They both equally alike felt to be perfect for each other. Yet they would not say it nor hint it, but they knew.

It was when they turned the last corner that Hannah recognized a car far ahead that she believed to belong to Kgomotso's parents. Every once in a while he drove it. His Parents had two more for day to day uses. It was only a matter of time before they made it officially his. He was their first born child and their only son. Both his siblings were girls.

Hannah had told him that every day she walked home from school with her friends and no one else. Friends Kgomotso had already passed along the way with his girlfriend nowhere to be seen. And had stopped to ask where Hannah was, and it was no surprise when it was Veronica who answered to tell him that Hannah was far behind them along the school route walking with a boy. The tall handsome young man drove off to find his girlfriend in gritted teeth.

Up ahead he recognized her and she the car, it had to be him inside, she knew that.

How would she avoid his quick resolve to violence now, she has given him more than enough cause. He once wanted to beat her up after seeing her hugging with a boy whom he later found out that was actually Hannah's cousin that she hadn't seen in a while, and to make the boyfriend even a bigger fool of himself; the cousin was a homosexual.

"Please act normal, okay?" She asked Patrick with her eyes still fixed on the car that had been reduced to a slow dramatic approach.

Patrick turned to her and asked "Normal? Haven't I been acting normal? And why should I 'act' normal?" But he needed not to be answered when he too could see the driver of the vehicle ahead.

Patrick's last night's thoughts about Kgomotso came to mind. He began to panic for he knew that if a fight was to break loose it would be one he'd have the likeliness of losing, no doubt about it. But no matter how terrified he was, he would not his fears bubble to the surface for her to see. On the outside he was calm, and she could see it in his eyes, how he intended to face the danger head on, she loved it, she loved him.

Facing oncoming traffic the car stopped right next to them and the driver looked through the rolled down window.

Looking first at Patrick he greeted only to assert dominance, addressed him as one would a little boy in exchange of greetings.
After Patrick greeted back Hannah peeked in and urged Patrick to walk on ahead without her.. "Go on without me, Patrick." She said, and had to walk round the car to get in and get that argument over with.
But Patrick had not liked how Kgomotso had just addressed him. He thought it would be fair to them both that he too does something to make him feel just as the way he just did if not more when he belittled him in front of her like that. He wanted to get even with him, a bold move for someone who would be at a great disadvantage should a fight break loose.

Quick on his feet he made haste to make it before her to the left front passenger door, he opened it for her with him seating there idle in the driver's seat. And just after he had closed the door gently he leaned in on her window, "Hey, don't be late tonight, I'll be waiting." He said, "Oh! And bring your books too. We might have to revise for the test a bit." He was purposely making it clear that the revision was not the main reason Hannah would be coming over to his place later on, and before getting up straight he glanced at the driver and he liked the look he saw in his eyes, anger. Gritted teeth and jaw muscles flexed. It was a sight that brought him satisfaction.
He walked the rest of the short walk home alone, but satisfied still...

An hour after he had got home he went to feed the puppies in the lab. He had to open the other sack of the dog food.
Once the pups were fed he carried them out the lab to play with them in the lawn.
But when he opened the front door with the cage by his side he saw Hannah not that far from the door and approaching *"She's early."* He thought shifting his eyes to the cage at his feet.

He attempted to look straight into her eyes as she approached, but she hid hers by gazing upon the ground before her. She only raised them to meet his when she got to the door.

Surprised he beat her to the first word "You're early."
"Yeah, the test is tomorrow." she said "I want to have everything covered when I leave tonight.
But Patrick thought the explanation did not really justify her early arrival for they only have so little work left that they haven't covered

yet for the upcoming test, so he replied "But we only have so little left to do."
"Okay Patrick, do I really have to spell it out?" She asked suggesting that there was an ulterior motive to her early arrival, just as Patrick suspected of course.
"Spell what out?" Patrick asked making way for her to get through the door.
Once Hannah was through the door Patrick pushed it close and followed her lifting the cage with both hands.

"Okay dumb Patrick." She amusingly addressed and began to explain herself "I wanna spend more time with you. Satisfied?" She turned back and found Patrick standing in front of the 'strange door' and got the impression that Patrick did not hear a word of what she just said. So she had to ask "Patrick, did you hear me?"
"Well I did hear you talk but I wasn't really listening, what were you saying again?" He asked making an idiotic face.
Hannah turned to walk into the TV room and said "Never mind, idiot." An idiot she couldn't get out of her thoughts. An idiot she just ended things with her boyfriend for. An idiot she loved.

Puppies locked away back into the lab he came into the TV room. When he knelt beside her she asked "What's that nice smell?" after sniffing the sudden refreshing odor in the air.

"It's the hand sterilizer from…the 'strange room'." He responded to her holding out his hands to her face to sniff more, but almost said lab in place of 'strange room' as Hannah called it.
"Wow! It smells nice. You like to keep clean, don't you?" She asked still sniffing the odor, and her question needed no answer. She never visited Patrick and found things untidy neither in the kitchen when she passed by it, nor in the TV room, and thought of the other rooms she hadn't yet explored to be in the same state, tidy.

"Well, let's just say moms taught me better before she…left." He said and once again almost said one word in place of another, 'died' in place of 'left'.
Hannah had to ask "Don't you miss her?"
"Who wouldn't?" he asked back and she would not reply back, she too missed her mother. The two had so much in common, both their mothers gone and their father's away.

When the time reached five O'clock the TV automatically switched itself ON and again automatically tuned itself to Patrick's favorite cartoons.
But she again wouldn't let him have it his way "Turn it OFF." she said commandingly with a stare at the wide screen ahead.
Patrick did not protest - he knew that it was no use to argue over it when he had the chance of catching the whole week's episodes in the omnibus on the weekend. And he didn't want to risk annoying her to a point of changing her mind about what's to follow after the math revision.

The sunlight through the blinds began darkening. The sun was getting low.
It was she who asked that they stop - they had covered the last part of the topics that will be in the test they were going to be writing in the following day to come. She wasn't confident that she was going to get the marks she aimed for in the test, she could've asked to revise some more, but she would not, her mind yearned for something else other than understanding the art of calculations, the art that seemingly came so easy to him.

"Turn the TV on." She said, "Maybe there's a nice movie playing." she sat comfortably on the couch, but all that comfort would crumble away when Patrick sat that close next to her. Yet she gave full attention to the TV ahead she had no sense of what was happening in the movie and her heart would almost stop when Patrick spoke with a whisper softly to her ear "Do I get to kiss you back for last night now?"
She turned and found his face terrifyingly close to hers, and would reply "If you want to." Her breathing had changed, he could hear her breathe. And when he'd tap his lips on hers it took the last of her breath away, he looked into her eyes before closing them to brush his lips on hers. Softly he pried her lips with his apart. Watching that romance movie was paying off. It seems everything Patrick does pays off in the end.
She held on to the back of his neck with both hands and started kissing him intensely, almost as if she had been longing to kiss him for some time like that, but oh! She has been. And he would kiss her more back. The boxer shorts under his polyester trousers would not hold his member down.
He began to do what he saw happen in the movie he watched last night during the kissing scenes. First he caressed her body with his hands as

he continued to kiss her, lowered them both to her her hips and began to pull her sweater up as to take it off and she was not against that. She even set her body right so it would be much easier for him to take the sweater off. In response she too began to hurriedly pull up his shirt with uncontrollable lusty desires arousing from her own thoughts of intimacy.
Her sweater was all the way up to the neck with the bra covering the perfectly round shaped breasts fully exposed when she slithered on top of him and felt the erect member press hard against the extreme inside of her right thigh over her blue jeans. She quickly pulled up her face to stop their over-affectionate moment.
They both opened their eyes and began to gasp for air. Patrick was lying on his back on the couch and Hannah was on top of him, she held him down by the chest with Patrick's lower body between her thighs with his shirt pulled up all the way to his neck and one arm already out.

When she looked straight down into his eyes and he straight up into hers, she asked "You're not ready for that, are you?"
"I guess I'm not." Patrick answered back knowing exactly what she referred to, he noticed that she felt it, his excited state.
She pulled back down her sweater and got off him to sit upright on the couch and he too set upright pulling his shirt back down. The silence felt to last forever with neither attempting to say a word, but you the way they sat awkwardly next to one another that they both wanted more, more of one another.
Patrick turned to her and finally spoke "But I'd like to learn, and from you."
"When do you want me to come over." She asked back not looking at Patrick who then found it much easier to look into her eyes while she was the one who was finding it hard to look into his. But she couldn't hide the smile that was visible from all directions. She had never felt such intensified lust for a boy before, not even for him - Kgomotso - in their two accounts of sexual intimacy.

"How about tomorrow evening?" he asked still with his sight fixed on her face. "Plus we won't have any school work revision then."
Hannah still not looking at Patrick just nodded to agree with her eyes fixed on the TV before them. She sought to understand what took her over, but the mysteries of love can never be that easy to unravel. She struggled to understand mathematics, how could she hope to

understand chemistry?
His eyes on the screen "I can't wait for tomorrow evening then." and asked "So what do we do now?"
"Now, I go home, we both have to sleep early we have a math test tomorrow, remember?" She said and stood to put her books back into her side back.

Patrick led the way to the front door. He opened the door and allowed her to go through first like always.
The horizon in which the sun set at was still a bit reddish, the sun had just set. The walk to the gate was a bit awkward as there was an unusual distance between them and silence mediated.
When Patrick noticed that Hannah was going to walk through her home gate without saying even goodbye he reached "You'll walk away just like that?" he questioned and hoped that she'd raise her eyes to him.
Hannah turned and walked into his chest and they both opened their arms to hug. She whispered in his ear "Goodnight, Patrick."

Patrick too said the same 'Goodnight, Patrick' to her before correcting himself to say "Goodnight, Hannah." but she did not pull out to walk away, she kept holding onto him as if listening and enjoying the thunderous beats of his heart, which kept racing.
"You can let go now." Patrick spoke softly into her ear that was that close to his mouth.
She pulled her head back and looked that deep into his eyes, for the first time since the kiss, and said "But I don't wanna let go." in a low voice.
Patrick lowered his hands to just above her rear end, looking back into her light brown eyes he said "That makes the two of us. But we have to if we want to do it again tomorrow." he was quoting her. His voice was slow and smooth, hypnotizing sound to her ears.

She raised her hands to the back of his neck and still looking into his eyes she suggested "One last kiss then."
Before Patrick could say a word, her lips were on his. And when they pulled out, Patrick could still taste them and feel their light clasp on his. She knew that was she to stand there with him any second longer it would extend into a minute and she'd never get to go, so, she let go of him and awaited him to do the same. He let go and watched her walk away, he missed her touch already...

The next morning Patrick overslept a little. The alarm clock did not go off, its batteries were dead. He even had to run to school to make sure to arrive on time.
He would not get to walk with her in the afternoon either; she had to leave school early that day. After break she got called to the principal's office, and came back ten minutes later, but only to get her school bag. Left the class without explaining herself to anyone, but to Patrick she said something. Before picking up her back pack with a lot of eyes on her she leaned into him and said "I've got to go, but I'll see you tomorrow about that thing." and without the slightest care of who was watching she kissed him on the cheek right there right then "I'll be missing you." She said and when he blushed horribly she stood back up and left the class followed by screams of adulations for what she just did, and Patrick was left to bask in the rest of it. How could every boy and girl in that class not envy to be them? They saw how he looked at her and how she looked back at him, they were in love, who wouldn't want to be?

Late afternoon just before sunset, Patrick was outside playing with the dogs when a car pulled up between the two houses, it was an SUV. A man he's never seen before got out of the driver's side to slide open the Motlhajwa gate. The car parked halfway to the porch and the two girls exited the car, Hannah and her younger sister, Portia. It was actually her who pointed out Patrick to her sister. Hannah shared everything with her, she was her best friend, of course she knew about the two. As soon as the man they came with disappeared into the house Hannah walked over to Mr. T's after pleading with her sister to keep watch for 'the man', and Portia would not let an opportunity to extort her sister for money pass her by, she kept watch.

The conversation between the two lovers was brief. Hannah explained herself, the reason she could not come to stay that evening.
'The man' was her father, a father that had not seen her daughters in over eight months. And a strict old schooled fellow of a man he was, he would not allow any of her daughters to be out after sunset, nor entertain the idea of any of them having a boyfriend while still in school.
Patrick understood, and knew that if it was he who had a chance to spend an evening with his father he'd choose it over anything and everything, except one though, the infinite project. That took priority that even seeing his father was not an exception.

When she least expected it Patrick stole a lightning fast kiss and when she stood love struck and pleasantly surprised Patrick began "You're the one always kissing me first." and added "Thought I should beat you to it this time."
"Then do it right." she said, hiding her eyes again.
"What if your father comes outside?" he had to ask, "There's no way he'll miss seeing us."
"I'm paying my security guard way too much for her not to tell me when my father is coming outside." She said.

Patrick took a glance at their lookout, she too turned to confirm that Portia was doing her job. When she turned back she found his face that close to hers, he's swift, and before she finished that thought his lips were heavy on hers. And when his manly arms wrapped around her with strong hands caressing her back she wished they were inside the house where no one would see them as she allowed him to take off all her clothes, because that's what she wanted him to do.
She had to stop the passionate moment, or the flames would burn too high to be doused and she'd have no strength to fight the urge to pull Patrick into the house. It took all out of her just to walk away and this time Patrick would not follow her to the gate.

"What is it?" she asked when she found her sister in radiant smiles.
"This one really loves you, sis." She said "Wish I had someone who admired me like that."
"How do you know he does?" She asked again, was it that obvious, she wondered.
"Well, he's still looking at you and smiling like an idiot." And asked "Is he like an idiot, I heard that every son of a teacher tends to be a slow learner, is that why you always go to him with books, to help him study?"
Hannah turned to Patrick and found him just as her sister had described him, all in smiles like an idiot. She blushed "And I love him too." She said, and quickly defended, "He actually helps me with school work. He's a genius, you know he never gets less than eighty percents in tests?" and added, "And you know what's weird, he never pays attention in class, doesn't take notes and in all the times I've visited him I've never found him studying he's always watching cartoons. He's a true genius. I've never met anyone like him. "
"Wow, sis!" she interjected the monologue that would have went on forever, "You really love him too, and way more than you did you know

who." She ended not mentioning Kgomotso's name, they had an agreement that his name would never be mentioned again, an agreement Hannah had to pay her younger sister for. Portia would never miss an opportunity to make extra money especially when it's off her own sister.
The two sisters walked holding hands into the house after Hannah had waved bye-bye to her admirer who lived in the house just across the street...

Saturday morning, a day he had promised to let her enter the strange room. He would finally make things right, tell her the truth where he had told her lies in the past. And finally ask her for that favor. He would need a qualified nurse in his project, and she would be the perfect choice, the only choice.

Again forgetting that there was no milk in the house, he pulled out the cereal box from one of the cupboards and put it on top of the kitchen counter. How could his memory fail him like that? He wondered. He decided that instead of going to the shop for milk, he'll have bread instead.
It was seventeen minutes before the animation omnibus when he finished his breakfast. And when he thought of the reason he had to miss some of the episodes during the week, he smiled, for he knew it was pleasantly worth it.

During the third episode of the omnibus he heard a knock at the front door. There was no question of the identity of the visitor in his heard. He knew exactly who it was, or rather had to be.
Before opening the door he took a deep breath and advised himself to relax, calm his heart down.
He pulled open the door, their eyes met. Without wasting a moment, he rushed to the first words, "Hey, I missed you." He said, "Wanna come in?" he asked already making way for her to come in.
"Of course, I wanna come in." she replied, "I missed you more. I wished I could have stayed a little longer yesterday."
"Well, you can stay a little longer today." he suggested, "I saw when I was playing with the pups outside that the car is gone."
"Yes, he had to leave early." she confirmed her father's departure, "He says he'll visit us again in the festive and would stay a few days then."

Unlike always, Hannah did not walk into the TV room. She stopped by the lab door, and Patrick almost bumped into her. "It's Saturday, is it not?" she asked. She was finally going to see what was behind the strange door. She looked into his eyes and saw hesitation, "Come on now, don't be changing your mind on me when I look so forward to this."
"I'm just scared that's all, scared that you might look at me differently after this." He spoke out, "Promise me you won't hate me." he pleaded. And when she saw how serious he was she knew that whatever it was behind that door had to be big, yet assure him "Patrick, there's nothing that can ever change how I feel about you." And had to ask "What are you hiding in there?"
"The real me." he answered sure of himself "And you might not like him as much as you like this pretence, this mask that I wear so well and often."
"Patrick, you're scaring me." she meant it, though would see that he was telling his truth when she looked into his dusty brown eyes. "Open the door already." She requested, hiding the terror of whatever that was to be discovered behind the heavy duty titanium door. Fear of the unknown, it gets to us all.

"But I wanna do something first." he delayed opening the door, "I might never get to do it again after today."
"Then do it already, I can't take the suspense of what's behind the door much longer." She said, "It's driving me crazy."
"You drive me crazy." He said. And before she would even think of a response her lips were engulfed in his. He kissed her with lusty urgency that only incited her ardent response. They stopped for a brief moment and Hannah backed into the wall, in shocking need of his kisses she pulled his face to hers as his body pressed her against the obstinate wall. His aroused body pressed hard against hers, a torch lighting the blaze swallowing her up in the inferno of passion. Hands began tugging at her tight jeans.
Then suddenly, from her back pocket, her phone began to ring irritatingly loud. "Don't stop!" she begged and he tried but the rings would not stop. They both halted out of breath.
It was Kgomotso calling, and what he wanted Hannah would not know for a while, because she did not answer it.
She adjusted her jeans avoiding his eyes. "This…will have to wait till

later." She said breathlessly, "How about we get to what I came here for." She added.

"I doubt you'll want to come into this house ever again after you walk out this room." Patrick mildly warned again, "What I'm about to tell you might...actually, will change how you think of me. And for what it shall be worth after this, I'm sorry for it all, and regret not telling you from the start." he added.
"What do you mean by that?" She curiously probed. She still stood with her back against the wall.
"Come see and hear for yourself." He said.
He unlocked the door, but did not push it open yet. He looked at Hannah and said "I wish I had done this sooner." before pushing open the titanium door.
Hannah walked through first and Patrick closed the door behind them.

As Hannah Paced around looking at the unfamiliar equipments that were in that room, Patrick began to tell her the truth - the whole truth. He began, "I did not live far from here before I came to live here, I lived with both my parents. The man you know as my father was just my primary school teacher at first, but by fifth grade he asked my parents to spend more time with me here in his house and they agreed. He became my mentor. Most of our time together we spent in this very room, with him helping me better my sharp intellect.
My mother did not leave us, she died when I was in seventh grade. And towards the end of that very year my father disappeared, he sold the house, took everything with him, left me behind with nothing except my birth certificate and a journal, his journal, with only three pages used, in a way explaining his disappearance." He continued as Hannah remained silent in disbelieve and shock. "When my father left that's when I came to live with Alfred who got arrested the same day I moved here, around the same time I met you. But all that, my mother's death, my father's disappearance, Alfred's arrest, never fazed me. My mind was wrapped around something bigger. That's when my actual work began. I questioned it all when my mother died, death, mortality, and Alfred answered every question the best he could. Everything has a loophole and I found it, the grey area between death and life. A way to cheat death, I found two." He went on to explain the two theories. Left nothing out, included the lizards, the dogs, how he caught them and his last experiment in detail as well as those that were to follow it, where the two pups would be the sacrificial test subject, for even he knew

there was no way they'd survive. The project was still in its early days for any of his test subject to live out the rest of its natural life span after the experiment. But the little he'd get should he perfect reattachment would be enough for him to keep chasing his goal. "When I start experimenting on actual people I'll need a nurse. And I want you to be it." he ended evenly.

Hannah just stood there shocked and out of words. And when she finally brought herself to speak it was to ask to leave, saying that she needed time to herself to process it all.
He tells her the truth, and the first thing she wants is to go home, get as far away from him as possible.
When he without protest opened the lab door for her and she walked to the front door, he did not attempt to stop her. He just followed her without saying a word still, his brain cells were working overtime to come up with words to try and make her understand. But she already did. What she did not understand was why she couldn't be angry or hate him for lying all these years. And she wanted to, hate him, be angry at him, but she couldn't, she loved him too much. And she knew firsthand the acts grief can push us to.

When they got to the gate, Patrick pulled her by the hand, "Will we be okay?" he asked, "I can't take losing you, I know this is too much. Please forgive me."
"Patrick, I've already forgiven you, I understand your reasons." She said looking less disturbed than she should have been, "But like you said, this is too much, so I don't know if we will be okay. I think it will be best if you give me some space to process it all." She made sense as she spoke but that doesn't mean Patrick liked what he was hearing.
"I meant it..." she looked steadily into his eyes, "Nothing will ever change how I feel about you, but I need time to take this all in. Will you be okay?" she cared, a tear escaped her left eye and another soon would her right eye and both were for him.

"Hey, don't cry." He said wiping the tears from her cheeks, "I can take the loneliness till you come around, I've been through worse, you know that now."
She planted her head into his chest and would not stop crying. His arms wrapped around her they stood there till she stopped crying.
She looked up into his worried eyes before kissing him one last time and thanked him for opening up to her, told him how much it meant to

her, that she appreciated it.
How long would it take for her to come around, what kind of time from him did she even need, would she no longer visit? What about in class at school, would they talk and if so how often and? He wondered as he watched her walk away with dried eyes.

Back into the house he began beating himself up, he was blaming himself for pushing her away, ironically, with the truth. He should've known, when you tell people the truth you can never know how they'll react to it. But he expected something like that for her reaction; to be honest even expected a little worse. Just that he did not know it would feel as it did.

He planted himself in the three-sitter couch and watched the last two episodes of the omnibus, but he couldn't help thinking that he had really lost her. He regretted having the idea of telling her the truth in the first place. Such thoughts made it even harder to enjoy those two back to back episodes of his favored cartoons.
That night, Patrick figured that the best way to deal with the situation was to do exactly what Hannah had asked of him - give her time by keeping away from her and eventually she'd come around, sooner rather than later, he desperately hoped.
Even though he went to bed late at close to midnight he found it hard to fall asleep, but eventually he did. And he wasn't the only one who struggled to find sleep that night. Hannah too found it hard to fall asleep. Her head convinced her of all the bad words she should have screamed at him. Words he surely deserved to be called.
But she did not hate him, she could not, she would not. And when she probed her heart and head alike for answers they both answered the same, 'you love him' and she agreed. Yet she could not understand why still.

CHAPTER SEVEN: Alfred's return

Patrick woke up in the not so late hours of Sunday morning regardless of the fact that he had slept pretty late last night.
After freshening up in the bathroom, he walked out the house and headed for the mini market. He wanted to have a big cereal breakfast that morning.
He would spend most of the day outside the house, hoping that she'd walk out her house and he'd see her. Thoughts of walking over to her house crossed his mind, but knowing that he'd most likely have to talk with whoever else he'd find in the house made him think otherwise.

Next morning, finally he had a chance to be with her as he saw her walk out the house at the same moment he did for school.
She greeted lowly hiding her face from his eyes. And she would surprise him after the formalities when she paced up to catch up to her friends who were just up ahead of them. She even asked of him to not speed up to walk past them.
In class she spoke to him, smiled at him and even laughed just enough to not give way to her friends the state of their relationship.
It took Patrick a few days to get used to it.
Every passing day meant a day closer to that day when things would get back to how they were between them before the truth speech, he remained equally hopeful as wishful.

Days came to pass; and they were that close to writing their prep exams.
On her birthday, the twenty fourth of August - it was on a windy Thursday. Hannah invited all of her friends and most of her classmates to her Aunt's house that late afternoon for some snacks and dancing to loud music. Her aunt had given her permission to do so, but Patrick wasn't invited, he was not surprised - given the circumstances. Yet Hannah when asked by her friends replied to say that she had invited him but he refused, he being him saying he did not want to be within a crowd, she explained. It raised no suspicion, they knew Patrick, and that sounded exactly like him.
After everyone had left, Hannah walked over with a large piece of cake to Mr. T's.

She knocked but got no answer back, yet would not leave. When she tested the door it gave way, and knew exactly where Patrick had to be. The titanium door was heavy but she managed, entered without him noticing. Found him right in his element. He was scribbling on the white board while in deep conversation with his-self. She could not keep up with what he was saying nor follow what he wrote on the board. A true genius at work, she admired and would not disturb.

When Patrick turned to revise notes from a notebook on top of the table behind him he found her there paralyzed in awe of what she witnessed.
"Hey, what are you doing?" He asked pleasantly surprised.
"Brought you cake." She answered and approached, "Remembered you have a sweet tooth and knew I had to save you some."
"Thanks, and happy birthday, again!" he said replacing the marker cap and when he turned back to her after putting the marker on its holder on the board he found her that close to him. "So how was the little party? Robert asked me if I was coming...told him that I had already explained to you that I couldn't."
"I told them something like that too." She said looking into his eyes with a gaze that said she longed for his touch, "To be honest, the party was boring, kept thinking of being elsewhere the whole time." she said evenly looking into his eyes with ease, "This was my most boring birthday ever."

Without even thinking about it his hands reached for her hips, "Come on, where else would you rather be than your own birthday party?" he probed.
She wrapped her hands around his neck, "Right here." She said and repeated "Right here with you, Patrick."
Patrick knew what was to happen next, but for some reason did not want it to go there. "Where's that cake you brought?" he asked removing his hands from her hips and maneuvered his neck out of her forearms. He headed for the lab door, she followed behind him.
After thanking her again for the cake he led her to the door, and would not walk her to the gate. He bid her goodnight once out the house and told her that he'd see her tomorrow in class.
He would not even bother to question himself of what he had just refused his-self. He went straight back to work in the lab, carried on from where he was interrupted, while Hannah would spend most of

the night wondering what had just happened, wondering why he'd deny her like that...

The following week on the same day - the thirty first of August, it was Patrick's turn to 'celebrate' his birthday. But Patrick did not have anyone to call a friend, so, he spent his nineteenth birthday no different to the previous four that came before it - all by his lonesome self. Coming to think of it, Hannah was older than Patrick - seven days older than Patrick to be precise. What fascinated Patrick even more was that their birthdays were always going to be on similar days, just seven days apart. He even confirmed it by skipping through the years in the TV's calendar checking those two specific days; the twenty fourth of August as well as the thirty first of that very same windy month of August. Whatever day Hannah's birthday would be on, His own would be too, just exactly one week later...

The preparatory examinations came and passed, and their end only meant the finals were nearing in. And they too would not be forever. They would pass, and Patrick's final academic year of high school would be done...
After the final examinations, Patrick couldn't wait to finally again have Mr. T in the house. His release day into house arrest was getting nearer and nearer with every sunset and sunrise. Mr. T had promised him that his experimentations will resume then - when he's back home.
But something else happened on the last day of the examinations. After the last exam of the year all the twelfth graders were at the peak of their individual joys except for Patrick who was in his usual drawn back from socialism personality. After the exam he went to lean against the tree he's been leaning against ever since his first day at Roseville High. It was most probably the last day that he would be doing that.
Hannah as she celebrated the last exam of her school days with her friends, classmates as well as grade-mates caught sight of Patrick leaning against that tree by himself with his eyes moving from one learner to the next. She kept turning her eyes to him from time to time for a while before deciding to go to him. They've been 'distant' long enough, she thought, especially after that night of her birthday.
When she got to Patrick's side he refused to make eye contact, then she asked "Still learning about human emotions?" her tone was mocking.

"Yeah, I kinda have to." Patrick replied with gritted teeth, "My life in a way depends on it, but you already know that, don't you?"

"Yeah, that I know." she affirmed, "So what are you learning right now, Patrick?" She inquired with curiosity, and this time followed Patrick's eyes with hers as they moved from one joyous learner to the next. Patrick began "I'd rather not talk about it, but all I can say is what you're all doing now ain't celebrating as you call it." he still would not turn to her, "Tearing-up uniforms? It's simply ignorance in its purest form, it's stupid don't you think?"
"Wow, you really are different." She observantly remarked, "How have you been, though?" and asked. Without noticing it, that she was revealing to him that she had actually missed him, that she still does. Patrick dipped both his hands into his trousers' front pockets "I can't complain, so I guess I've been fine." His voice was low and his response premeditated, "It was really nice, you leaving your friends to come to me all the way over here." He said taking a peek into her eyes that still searched for his, and turned away almost immediately, "But I've got to go home."

But before he could walk away Hannah stopped him, "Wait, since you talk of how we are so confused of what celebrating really is, how about you show me what celebrating really is." Patrick turned to her and didn't bother to mask his disinterest, "I can come by later in the afternoon, if you're not busy." She added, and there it was again, that provocative smile.
He looked straight into her eyes, and he couldn't believe how much he so wanted to kiss her, right there right then. "You of all people should know that I'm always busy. I doubt I'd have the time to do anything that does not contribute to my goal." He began with that serious voice of his, and spoke slowly as to ensure that the girl before her got the message behind every word vibrated into her ears, "So I have to say no to that offer and I'm not sorry about it, stay well, Hannah." He walked away without even waiting to hear her response or whether she bid him a farewell or not. He could survive and get by just fine without her in his life, his life before meeting her and the last three months had been sufficient proof of that.

Patrick had a chance to get close to her again, but he strongly refused it without even giving her the doubt that he might change his mind over time. What was this? What he's been hoping for everyday in the past few months comes to pass and he strikes it down without hesitation? Something was definitely going on in his complex head...

Weeks passed, and over these weeks Patrick and Hannah had seen each other only a few times regardless living just across the street from one another. Those times were when Patrick went to the mini-market or when he was out playing with the then a bit grown dogs in the lawn. Those two were just about the only times Patrick got to spend more than three minutes in the vicinity of the eyes of others - he spent an 'unhealthy' amount of time within the walls of the house, and most of it he'd be in the lab if not watching cartoons or movies and at times wild animals' documentaries on the satellite television.
Whenever they saw each other, Patrick and Hannah, there was no exchange of words, because Patrick every time gave Hannah the impression that he did not want to talk to her nor see her. He was treating Hannah no different to how she treated him after the whole truth speech that Patrick gave her. But it was not retaliation, it was definitely something else.
It obviously seemed that Hannah wanted things to go back to how they were between them just prior the revelation.
Patrick admitted to loving her, so much. He only distanced himself to avoid being loved back by her. He had convinced himself that he would not let her waste her love on him, that he did not deserve it, and that he was not worth it. But it was too late for that. She already loved him dearly, with every fiber of her being she believed.

One afternoon when Patrick was headed for the shop Hannah walked out her house too. There was no escaping for him this time, their paths were meant to once again cross.
When they walked out the gates almost at the same time Hannah stole a glance at him, but he still wouldn't look up at her. Her cute nose stuck in the air she asked "Where are you going?" She so longed to hear his deep thick voice.
"I'm going to the shop." Patrick replied lowly.
"I'm headed that way too." She said, and neared him. "Can we talk?"
"Hannah, I don't think that's a good idea." He said quietly.
She had to ask, "But why? Why are you doing this to me?" She knew that Patrick was definitely avoiding her. She couldn't understand why.
"Hannah, what you want I cannot give. I'll always put you second to my work. Do you want that? To be put second?" He asked, and would add before she'd reply, "You deserve more than that, you deserve more

than me." He still refused his eyes to look at her and not out of being shy, "I cannot give you all that you deserve." He ended coldly with his eyes minding his every step like he was walking on a ledge.

"I already know that." She said "But I don't mind that, Patrick." She continued "Can't you see that I miss talking to you? I miss you, Patrick. Don't you miss me?" Her eyes filled with the salty fluid that gave them the shine that the scowl faced boy bothered not to gaze upon.
"You know what, I change my mind." He tilted his head, and his eyes met hers. He missed looking upon that beautiful face. When he stopped she stopped too. "I'll go to the shop later on when you're nowhere to be seen." And with a grin he added soothingly "By the way...I do miss you too, Hannah, so much it hurts me to have to do this. Have a nice one now." He turned back home without waiting to hear what she had to say next.
Hannah continued the slow walk alone and couldn't hold her tears in.

Part of him wanted to stop all this madness, of course, but he had convinced himself that getting any closer to her would only lead to one of them hurting if not both of them in the end.
He hadn't seen his father or heard from him in over five years, but his words still influenced his decision making mechanism in a big way. The suffering that his father's journal warned about, he couldn't stop thinking about it. The journal made more sense now...

With only a day away from Mr. T's release into house arrest, Patrick made sure that everything was in order. He had tried his best to put his whole work regarding his ultimate goal in a way that it would be easier for Mr. T to understand, when he updated him.
The lab coats were clean and back from the dry cleaners, hung by the lab door. The dogs were both ready for experimentations.
Patrick had also made sure that the room in the garage that would be Mr. T's bedroom was in order with his thing placed smartly in it. Even the correctional officials that came by a month ago and again just a week ago to evaluate the environment, praised Patrick saying that he really was holding up real good by himself with his 'father' in prison.

That night before the mentor's release, Patrick went to sleep early so that he'd wake up early and have the early morning hours before Mr. T arrived, to make sure everything was still in order. He wanted everything to be perfect when Mr. T got back home to his house.

Nineteen December 2017 - release day for Alfred M. Tobetsa, into house arrest. That Tuesday morning Patrick woke by the sound of his alarm at five thirty, but the schools were closed for end of year - he went back to sleep and woke at eight thirty.
After his filling breakfast he began to recheck if everything was still as he had left it last night. He checked the interior of the house as much as he did the exterior.

By eleven thirty, his patience as to when Mr. T would arrive, had worn off. He kept going outside the house as to check if it was Mr. T or not whenever he heard the slightest sound of a car passing by.
Tired and starved from the ups and downs he's been doing he made himself a large spaghetti meal, but before munching down on it he made sure to feed his lab dogs. You'd think Alfred being the adult, he'd talk Patrick out of the madness. but no, he actually encouraged it, said he'd like to see it work one day. and Patrick aimed to impress.

When he came to eat his meal he did not bother to go outside to check if it was Mr. T or not whenever he heard the sound of a car driving by outside. He remained seated in the couch watching cartoons till he heard one sound of a car that sounded pretty close to the house. He got so convinced that it was Mr. T that he put his half eaten spaghetti bowl on the table and stood to go check.
Before opening the door he held on to the door knob without turning it and said "Here goes everything." silently to himself.
When he opened the door he found a blue police vehicle with its engine turned OFF halfway between the gate and the front door. He did not hesitate to approach the car. He stood a couple of meters away. But for a moment that felt like ages to Patrick, nothing happened. His excitement got the better of him, he couldn't take the suspense. He got even nearer the car and tried to see through the dim windows.

Only a hand reaches away from the driver's door, the dimmed window rolled down. Immediately when the face of the police officer on the driving side met Patrick's the officer greeted, "Good day young man."
"Good day indeed, sir." Patrick greeted back already trying to see who else was in the car, but he couldn't tell if there was anyone in the rear seats or not. The vehicle had a barrier between the front seats and the back seats. He could only make the woman in formal clothing who sat in the front passenger seat next to the police officer.

"What's your name, young man?" The officer asked.
Patrick thought first, "'Young *man!*'" and responded "My name is Patrick, Patrick Mot, sir."
"Okay then." Began the square jawed police officer with blue eyes that went pretty well with his white pale face, "Let's get this over and done with, shall we?" He turned his gaze briefly to the women seated next to him as he spoke. But she said nothing back.
The police officer asked Patrick to take a step back so he won't be hit by the car's door as it opened.
Both the woman and the husky officer got out the car. He first took in a deep breath and sighed out with his hands on his hips and his nose sticking in the air, he was a proud policeman. Too proud, Patrick observed. The officer turned to open the back right door of the car. He wore the same clothes he was arrested in five years ago. But to him it felt like he's been away for an eternity.
After Mr. T greeted Patrick addressing him as 'son' the four walked into the house. And Alfred nodded in acknowledgement as he scanned the yard that looked way better than it did back before prison. And he would be equally impressed when he found the inside of the house orderly neat, even wanted to ask the lad if he had hired a maid in his absence.

The conditions of his house arrest were made very clear to him, as well as to Patrick so that he could remind Mr. T what he stood to lose shall he be tempted to break any of the stipulations. He was fitted with an ankle monitor, a tracking devise around his ankle which will alert the correctional department the instant he takes a step beyond his barriers. After they explained to him that he was not to leave the yard or tamper with the tracker for that will only lend him back in prison the police officer and the woman left, after making Mr. T sign the final documents of his release into house arrest for the next five years. Patrick was requested to sign as well, as a witness.

In Prison Alfred had made a freedom list in his head. A list of all the things he'd want to do as soon as he got out of prison. So when he got out of prison five years earlier it was only expected that he attended to those items, especially the ones that did not violate his house arrest rules. But surprisingly he would not. The first thing he wanted to do as soon as his home escorts left, was enter his house lab.
Alfred nagged the young man who's lived under his roof for the last five years for progress in his project thus far. A project that involved

killing the pets they abducted and hoping to bring them back to life again, with their heads switched! How sick was that? How sicker were the people who went through with such plans?
Chances were that had he not been under house arrest he'd still not take that slow free roam around Roseville, in his car - driving a car was what he yearned for most while inside.

Alfred met the dogs, "I think they bite!" Patrick warned, "Grab a chair. You'll need it for this." He suggested and handed him both files of his two major theories.
The 'second theory' file was much bigger than the 'first theory' file only because he's been working mostly if not totally on 'second theory'.
They went through the files together with Patrick explaining things only here and there because most to Mr. T were easy to understand.
After the two went through Patrick's progress Mr. T told Patrick of all of the new technological equipments they will need to conduct productive experiments. He even made a list, one that looked no different to a grocery shopping list.
"We should get all this within a month." began Mr. T, "Only if you could drive we'd be able to get them that fast, but using store deliveries…it would take at least three months to get everything on this list." He handed the list to Patrick, "And longer if there'll be international importations required." He added.

Patrick stood and said "You're still living in the past, T." He exited the lab.
When he walked back into the lab a minute later, he had with him his laptop. On it, he signed in into a website called takealot.com.
"You just have to place your orders in here, contact details here and your address as well, and the products will be delivered in a week if no international importation is needed." Said Patrick while showing Mr. T how easy and quick it will be to get all the equipments they needed, he tried his best to sound smart. But he needed not to try that hard, that man beside him already knew how smart Patrick was.

"You bought a laptop, nice. Can't wait to see what else you've been spending my money on, or even who?" he said sardonically, but he wouldn't have to worry, Patrick had actually been smart with his money. Alfred would be surprised when he realizes that Patrick had not even spent a tenth of what he had expected an unsupervised

teenage boy to spend in five years.
With the laptop Patrick introduced Alfred to Takealot.com.

After Patrick had placed the order, the two began to catch up on lost years. It was a conversation Patrick once dreamt of having with his own father. Didn't his own father miss him? He wondered sometimes. Mr. T did not disagree with Patrick when he told him that he did not want to acquire a higher education certificate. That he did not want to go to a tertiary institution.
He only advised him that it would be best if he had something to fall back on, a job; a career when what he hoped to achieve failed. But in response he said that there was no way what he hoped to achieve would fail, he added on to say that the only way he'd ever stop working towards his goal was if he died before he finishes it. "What use would qualifications to a good job be if I'm dead?" He murmured silently. And Alfred didn't want to try and speak some more sense into him. All that he wanted to do was help him to his best abilities and resources to get even closer to that farfetched idea of immortality.

The two left the lab when Mr. T at last suggested that it was time he saw his new room, and he was also tired. The excitement of going home had kept him up in the last two nights.
He wanted to take a long bath. In prison, over the years he's been only taking showers, there are no bath tubs in prison.
But first Mr. T asked Patrick to log into a few online banking accounts, three actually. It's then that Patrick came to realize where the money that was being deposited monthly into Mr. T's bank account had been coming from.
The judge's sentence, five years ago, was harsh. But because Mr. T had a 'son' that depended solely on him for sustenance, the judge saw it unfair to punish him for his father's crimes. None of his accounts were frozen.
Mr. T was really a genius who planned for the stormy days. Through his teaching years he's been saving fifty percent of his monthly net salaries, and two years prior to his arrest he bought small shares in three companies that showed good promises of big returns. The total returns by then from those shares were more than enough capital to fund the whole of Patrick's project from scratch including all high tech equipments that were yet to be bought, and also pay for the nurse that Patrick was yet to tell Mr. T about.

Earlier that night Patrick went to knock at Mr. T's new bedroom to tell him that supper was ready. This time he had added something to his menu - he did not only mix his boiled spaghetti with tomato sauce, he also mixed in baked beans and mixed vegetables. Mr. T too was a fan of spaghetti, but did not prefer to have it as frequently as Patrick did. The two enjoyed their meal seated round the dinner table, and constantly broke into humorous topics that the imprisoned party kept initiating.

After the meal they one after the other went to take quick baths, and after Patrick did the dishes he came to join Mr. T who was watching a TV show in the living room. Patrick had to accompany his hysterical laugh with a question of what was his mentor thinking immediately when he caught on to the title of the series Alfred was attentively watching, 'Prison Break.' But he wasn't planning anything like that. He used to watch that same show before he went to prison.
Mr. T left to sleep in his new comfortable bed around midnight. Patrick watched one last movie by himself before he too retired to the four walls that were his bedroom...

"And here I thought I was the only early riser." Alfred began at Patrick as he walked round the house to find him playing with the dogs on the recently trimmed grass, "Aren't you getting too attached to them?" he asked, "You're aware that we are going to decapitate them as soon as the equipments arrive, right?"
Patrick called the dogs to him and bent down to pet them both. "I've done this before, T." he said tonelessly, and asked "How was your first night back home?"
"It was the best yet, I slept like a baby on sleeping pills." He quickly replied, "I'm starved! What's for breakfast?" asked, and wouldn't get any closer to Patrick, because of the dogs that felt the need to defend him, from the middle aged man who stood before them.
"There's plenty of cereal, but I'm out of milk." He replied, "But I could go to the shop for some, maybe even bread, some eggs, and everything else to make it a big one."
"Fine with me." said Alfred, "Your cooking last night wasn't bad, I'd like to see what you're capable of when it comes to breakfast." He added both daring and urging Patrick on. Patrick rushed to the mini market and was back in no time. The two had the biggest breakfast Patrick has ever made. And Alfred didn't hold back on the praises of the young boys cooking skills. He has had enough practice with those specific ingredients.

After the big breakfast, no time would be delayed on anything else other than the one thing they both equally regarded priority, the lab works.
That day's discussion was the need of an actual medical doctor and a nurse. Even Patrick admitted that some things without proper medical training would be beyond him. He had to convince Alfred that they should hire a doctor in the later stages of the project; a doctor that will work strictly under them. But Alfred surprised him when he argued and refused the idea. And when he explained his reasons to him, the young man saw it the old man's way.
"But we still need to have an MD, someone with proper training." He said, "And if we can't hire one, well, the last option is for one of us to become an MD." Even his face showed that it was a move he never actually thought it would come to making.

"Don't look at me. I'll be under house arrest for the next five years, or have you forgotten already?" Mr. T reminded with a humorous tone and quickly added "But we have you. I bet your grades are good enough to apply to a medical school and you haven't applied to any institution, so...why don't you do it, Patrick?"
Patrick did not protest the idea, he looked steadily back at Alfred and began affirmatively "If I have to...for the project I'll do it, but that means you'll be all alone in this house for the next seven years, or more.", he continued "You can't walk out the yard for the next five years, so what happens when you need something from beyond the fences? But..." He raised his index finger before Mr. T could respond, "I think I have an idea that might be a solution to your confinement, but you might not like it."

"Well, let me hear it first." He said "And I'll decide for myself if I like it or not."
Patrick looked at him and smiled before saying "I'm getting you a babysitter, you..."
But Alfred interrupted, loudly! "What?" and continued to argue the idea "No, that ain't happening. Firstly I can sit myself, and secondly...I am not a baby, Patrick." There was humor in his response but he stood firm by it.
Patrick wouldn't let him shoot it down just like that, without letting him hear reason, "Yeah, I hear you, so hear me out too. The person whom I'll give the post of the nurse...that's the person whom I'll ask to come once in the afternoon on weekdays and twice on weekends, in

the morning and the afternoon, we need her, but it's mostly you who needs her for now, I'm not leaving for medical school if it means you'll be left here by yourself." he paused to add "We really need this one, T." But something else was fueling his interests, other than the fact that Hannah had always wanted to be a nurse from a young age.

"Okay." He affirmed only because it made sense, "I'm doing it because you say we need this nurse." Mr. T agreed but he was noticeably not a hundred percent onboard with the idea.
Patrick looked at him as if hiding something and said "There's something else, she's not a nurse..." and quickly added refusing Mr. T to say anything before him "Not a nurse yet! That's how we'll pay her for helping you out in the next five years. We'll fund her nursing studies and give her a little extra on the side for pocket money."
"What?" Alfred uttered confused, "Tell me you're joking, Patrick." He said, "Because if you're serious, then I'm not doing it." He stressed, "I'm not having a teenage girl play maid in my house."
It was in that moment that Alfred would witness a side of Patrick he had not known, a side that clearly stated that he was not a mere boy anymore but a young man. "This debate is taking us nowhere." He began firmly his voice deep and unmasked, "Alfred, you've got three choices...each got its own side effects. One, we don't get you a helper and I don't go to medical school because I won't leave you here alone, so we have to hire a medical doctor. Two, we hire a helper you'd like and I go to medical school, but the helper might not be a nurse and even if she is she might not agree with the lab works, so we'll spend more time looking for an actual nurse whom will agree with the lab works and we'll have to risk them not keeping everything a secret, a big risk. Or you let me get you the helper I have in mind and I go to medical school, when I come back she'll already be a nurse and she already proven to have interest in the lab works and I trust her to keep it a secret." He spoke boldly "So quit arguing and choose. I'm okay with any choice you make." Even though he had not raised his voice when he spoke, Alfred still felt the crushing weight of it. The tables seemed to have turned, Alfred a student and Patrick a teacher that had had enough of his objections, so Alfred felt.

"You really are his son." He said in full recognition of the young man Patrick was. "He will be proud." He ended masking his own pride.
"Choose, Alfred!" he urged him on, "We don't have all day."

"Okay Patrick, we'll do it your way." He said and quickly added "But don't make me regret it."
"You know I'll do my best not to." He replied, and meant it.
Admiring the young man, "This side of you...you just showed and all to get this specific person in here, you must really like her." He gazed upon Patrick with curious eyes that sought to know more of the mysterious young lady "Who is she?" and thought she brought out the best in him, he was now a man and he needed someone like that in his life. He for one knows what it's like to have someone like that in your life, and knows in the most painful way what it feels like to lose them in the end. He wished that would never come to Patrick.
"You'll see soon enough." Said Patrick, and stood to approach the lab door leaving Mr. T alone to go through the data collected on the two theories of attaining immortality one more time by his-self.
Out the titanium lab door he peaked in, and spoke humorously "Let me go get you a sitter." He then added as if advising a toddler "Don't break anything, now!" and pulled close the door before Alfred could respond.

Patrick absent mindedly walked to the gate, and almost did not see the dogs follow him, he turned and ordered them to stay, and they obeyed. Out the yard he walked to the Motlhajwa residence gate. When he got to it he stopped, "This better work." He silently said to himself. He tested the gate, it was unlocked. He slid it open and walked through that gate for the first time in his life.
As he walked to the door his breathing changed, he started fiddling with his wrist watch, the panic set in swiftly.
He got to the door way before he could finish devising a plan of exactly what he'll say to her.
Before knocking he almost changed his mind, but he went through with it.
After the third knock someone opened the door, but it was not who he expected.
He had to greet first, "Hi Portia...is your sister here?"
"Hello, Patrick" She greeted back, "Yes, she's inside, should I call her for you?"
Patrick without hesitation replied to say "Yes, please." He was still fiddling with his watch, trying to figure out how he'd say what he had come to say.
But Portia before turning to disappear into the inside of the house felt the need to ask and confirm "Is it true that you're a genius?" she looked

steadily into his eyes and searched to see who he truly was, "She talks about you a lot, too much sometimes."

"Not a genius, I'm just addicted to the employment of logic." he answered, "Who even told you that I am."
"The same person you're here for." She replied "Like I said, she talks about you a lot. Guess she wasn't lying, you do sound like a genius. She is lucky."
"*It's actually the other way around.*"Patrick thought to himself as Portia disappeared back into the house and came back leading Hannah to the door.
It was Hannah who greeted at first sight, Patrick just nodded back and waited for Portia to turn back but she did not.
He began "I need to talk with you." He shifted his eyes to the younger sister and asked softly "Hey Portia, can you please give us a minute alone, please." and she would not protest, her sister will tell her everything later at night anyway, she knew.
Right there in the veranda there were two benches, Patrick sat on one and asked Hannah to sit on the other.
"Nursing school next year?" He asked, and still would not let go of his watch.
"Hopefully, yes." She replied optimistically, "I'm still waiting for any of my bursary applications to be successful, why are you asking me this, if I may ask?" She wondered.
Patrick tilted his head to look into her face, she was still the most beautiful girl he's ever seen, "Well, I've sat next to you the whole year, so I have an idea of where your grades stand, and we both know they are not at a standing where they stand a good chance of snatching a bursary." He paused before asking, "Can you afford to pay for yourself? At any higher education institution I mean, for your nursing course?"

"Well, it will stretch my aunt's budget, but it can be afforded, plus the local nursing school here in Roseville is not that expensive, and I won't be needing any unnecessary expenses like transport for starters, I mean I'll be living right here at home, it doesn't get cheaper than that." Then she asked "Why are you asking me all this, Patrick?"
"Still curious I see." He drew a current of air in and out to explain himself, "Remember what you saw back in my 'evil lair'?" A brief sinister smile escaped his face, "I still want you to be the nurse. Alfred got back from prison yesterday, but he's under house arrest, he can't leave the yard, I'm going to medical school myself next year and he'll

be all alone. He'll need someone who'll check on him once on weekdays and twice on Sundays and Saturdays, to get him things he'll need from beyond the fences. I want that person to be you still. He has already agreed to the idea. And as for your payment...your whole nursing course will be paid for and you'll also be given pocket money on the side of course. So, will you take the offer?" He waited anxiously for a yes.

"Wow, that's so human of you Patrick, but I won't take it." She declined the offer without even thinking about it much. It was clear that certain emotions were in play.
Patrick had to ask "But why?" and added "It's the best offer yet, if not, tell me what more you want and I'll make it happen."
She replied shocked that Patrick even asked, "Really Patrick? Not so long ago you didn't want to talk to me, let alone be anywhere near me, you made that very clear, remember? Find someone else."

"But I don't want someone else, I want you, Hannah. Please take the offer." Patrick pleaded, "I really need you." He murmured softly beside her and repeated "I need you."
She could hear in his voice how sincere he was, "I'll think about it, but I don't think I'll change my mind." She said evenly, "So please, don't be holding your breath, okay?"
After Patrick told her that he had said what he wanted to say, the two stood and Patrick walked to the gate leaving Hannah standing in the veranda still puzzled by just the kind of person Patrick was, and the offer just confounded her even more. *"You love him."* Her heart softly spoke to her stubborn head still, and no amount of confusion would change that...

Over the dark complexion Alfred could see clearly the shade of disappointment on his face, but asked regardless "So when is the sitter coming?" he sought not his eyes and added "I can't wait to meet her."
"I don't know, maybe never." Patrick replied, "And it's my entire fault that she might never come. How do I make my own decisions when all I can think about is what he wrote in that journal? Wish I never read it."
"Don't look so down, it will work out." Alfred began, "It doesn't have to be the special mystery lady of yours...you can always find another sitter."
Patrick slowly turned to raise his eyes to him, in that instant, Alfred knew, what he said had angered the boy. "But I don't want another! I

want her, why can't you both get that!" He said angrily, but he would not raise his voice to his mentor nor reveal the full magnitude of his anger and disappointment to him, "I don't care anymore about the sitter, it's totally up to you who you hire." There was that familiar scowl on his face again, "But as for the nurse, it's either we have her or no nurse at all." He dragged his feet to walk to his bedroom, and it was clear what he'd do when he gets there. Think critically on his next move...

It had been over two hours, and Patrick still hadn't come out of his bedroom. Alfred had been sitting patiently in the TV room waiting for him walk out, had already even played out in his head the little conversation he'd have with the young man to cheer him up or at the least help him accept what was and look forward to what could be.

Just as he was getting sleepy on the couch, he heard the faint knock at the front door, heard it over the sound of the loud television before him. '*Maybe it's a neighbor here to welcome me back.*' He thought as he stood to the door with a stretched yawn. When he opened the door, the face behind it was not of a known neighbor, but in a way it was rather familiar. "Good day sir." The young lady greeted first.
Mr. T greeted back still puzzled at who the girl could be when she looked so familiar, it couldn't be any of the kids he taught in primary school before being arrested. Patrick was the only one he was social with. It's only when she told him where she lived that he remembered her.
Funny thing, he remembered her as the girl who he once told Patrick about back in the day of his arrest.
"Wow, Brenda's niece, Hannah, right? You really have grown into a beautiful young woman, haven't you?" Mr. T complemented and a smile escaped Hannah's face, "What brings you across?" he asked.

"I'm here to see Patrick." She answered, "Is he home?"
"Yes, he is home." He continued "He locked himself in his room a while ago to sulk away. I think someone kind of...broke his heart!" He whispered the 'broke his heart' part.
Hannah knew that that someone was most likely to be herself.
Mr. T thinking the same thing asked "It's not you, is it?" and when he noticed her shy her face away with guilt, he needed not to ask again or await her response. It was clear that she had something if not everything to do with Patrick's sudden change of mood. Patrick must

have taken the advice to befriend Hannah to the next level, so Alfred figured.
"I'll go get him for you, do come in." Mr. T invited her in. Hannah followed Mr. T through but stopped in the TV room to take a seat on the couch she had her intensified kissing moment with Patrick. It brought back memories. She remembered it like it had happened just yesterday, and the deeper she drifted into memory lane the more real his imaginary lips felt on hers, she even closed her eyes for a brief moment, opening them as soon as she thought of how silly she must have looked right then. How could she feel like that about him and still bring herself to be the one to disappoint him like that? Because that was what she had come to do, disappoint him, she had come to tell him that she could not accept the offer he made her earlier on, but would she, now that Alfred had made her aware of the state she had already put him in with just a maybe. Saying 'no' to him would definitely break him two times over if not more, which was likely.
Her heart spoke softly to her yet again "*He loves you too.*" She believed it "*Just as much as you him.*" it added.

Slowly behind Alfred Patrick followed into the TV room with one hand pinching his wrist, just where the wrist watch would be. He had taken it off when he threw himself on the bed.
Immediately after Patrick sat down Alfred began "I guess this is my cue." And walked towards the door that opened to the backyard, when he got to the door he turned and warned with a humorous stare at the young lady "And don't do anything funny with him." he pulled the door shut behind him.
Patrick looked across to her and would not hesitate, or hide his frustration from her "So what did you decide?" he asked, "Are you going to take the offer or not?"
"Yes. I'll take the offer." She answered evenly, "But there's one huge condition." She added unflinchingly.
"Let's hear it." he said, "And let it be something doable, please."

"Never lie to me again, or push me away." She said, "It hurts more when it's from the people you love." There! She said it, and he heard it loud and clear.
"Of course, I'll never do that again." He assured, and stood from the couch only to come sit next to her, "I promise, if anything, I'll pull you even closer to myself." he ended.
"Why were you even doing it?" she asked, her face that close to his, "It

didn't make any sense why you'd push me away like that all of the sudden, so why did you do it?"
"I was scared." He answered truthfully, "It scares me that I'm gonna lose everything I hold dear to myself one day, this place I call home, these ideas that help me look forward to tomorrow, Mr. T, the only man who gives me the taste of fatherly love, and the one thing I hold most dearest above all, my life. Hannah, it scares me to think that I can lose it all just like that, in an instant. I so didn't want to add you to that list, but it's too late now." his hand reached for her left cheek, "One more person to my list, you. I thought 'you can't lose something you don't have.' If I didn't have you, I couldn't lose you. That's why I pushed you away, to not have you. But the harder I pushed it became more clear that I already..."
But Hannah would not let him finish. She placed her index finger on his lips and leaned in to whisper "You don't need to say it, I know, I can see it in your eyes, remember? The eyes never lie." she substituted her index finger with her lips. They were once again kissing - on the very couch they had their first real kiss - the technical first can be ignored. When they stopped, she looked deep into Patrick's eyes with her face that close to his and said "It's okay to be scared, Patrick, it only makes you more human."
Patrick pulled further back and asked "Wait, does that mean we can be boyfriend and girlfriend now?"
"Yes, Patrick!" She answered with a laugh. "We can be boyfriend and girlfriend now." she leaned in and kissed him some more.
Without struggling to part their lips, he spoke "But I might be leaving in a few weeks for medical school, and if I do I'll be gone for seven full years or more if necessary."
"For you, I'll wait." Hannah responded without even the slightest doubt in her mind. "Just promise me that you'll come back." She whispered softly into his face and kissed him again "Promise you'll come back to me."

After the passionate moments, their faces still remained that close to one another.
"Now I just have to tell my aunt about the offer, I'm pretty sure she won't disagree." Said Hannah, she continued playing with the lobes of his ears in a caressing manner. "But she might want to talk to Alfred first, you know how adults are." She kissed Patrick on the chick before standing to walk to the front door.

Out the door they walked holding hands. When they got to her home gate, Patrick did what he hadn't had the chance to do in a pretty long time - he protested to let her go. He pulled her towards himself and they hugged, then he let her go after the last brush of her lips on his. He watched as she walked through the gate and straight to her front door...

More than a week after Mr. T's return, all equipments they've ordered on 'takealot.com' were delivered. Mr. T was so impressed with the products and the delivery service all the same. He even gave the delivery man a tip, a big one.
On the twenty seventh of December, Patrick spent the whole day in the lab with Mr. T testing the new equipments with the aid of the manual books. And later that day he went to hook up with Hannah whom was then his official girlfriend - his first, at the age of nineteen. The two spent the whole afternoon till sunset at the local park. MANBEAST Park had a carnival that day. Magicians and circus performers were in town. It was not a surprise for every young couple in Roseville to be there that day. Even Kgomotso was there, with his new girlfriend...

On the eve of the New Year, Patrick and Mr. T got to use the newly bought equipments in an actual experiment. The two dogs were the test subjects in Patrick's 'second theory' experimentation.
Both dogs died, but great progress was made regardless the deaths. They were able to keep one of the two dogs barely alive for two more minutes with its head severed from the body. One of the new machines could easily read the faintest signs of life.
That interval of life was what they had to elongate to get that window for reattachment of the substitute head in their next experiment.

Alfred with the aid of his resume, his long list of college friends in high places and Patrick's grades was able to get the young man accepted in one of the best private medical schools within the country. He had wanted him to go abroad, but all applications for abroad enrolments for the 2018 academic year were already closed.
Patrick left for medical school on the fifteenth of January 2018, that day was the day he got to do the hardest thing by far - say goodbye to his first and only girlfriend. He even shed a tear. And when Hannah embraced him in her arms, he too held on tighter, but sadly; only to let go.
He was going to be away for seven years or more if needed be, and in

that time he would not see either Hannah or Mr. T - he had decided that he would not come back even just to visit till he completed his studies. He did not want to bare another moment of having to say goodbye to her.

But who was he kidding? Staying away for that long with how he felt about her would be close to impossible, if not the word itself...

CHAPTER EIGHT: Alfred critical

It was on the third year of his studies, towards the end of the first semester of that year, that he decided he would visit Roseville. Emotionally distant as he was, he admitted, but only to himself, that he missed her! The longing to see her ran deed. In the last six months up to then, Patrick had desired nothing more than to look upon her beautiful face, to look into her mesmerizing eyes once again. To hear that one distinct laugh of hers only he possessed the whimsical ways to conjure up into existence. To be so close to her that he'd fear that she would hear his galloping heart that raced into the uncharted territories of complex emotions, erotic desires. And only had he sat to consider her emotions and thoughts; that she missed him too as much as he did her if not more, he would have visited back home sooner, rather than wait for more than two years to finally make the simple effortless decision - catching a bus.

"*A week would suffice.*" He thought and believed.

His winter holidays would be a month long. Exactly four and a half weeks before the start of his second and last semester of his third academic year.

Back in Roseville, the only two people who mattered to him, had only expected him to return after the completion of his course, just as he had made it clear to them before he left more than two years ago. But it didn't mean they didn't long to see him anytime soon, especially '*his*' Hannah, whom then had completed her nursing course and was a fully qualified and practicing nurse. She had finally stepped into the massive, but comfortable shoes of the woman she looked up to, the long gone Alice Mot. The woman she still had not learnt to be the mother of the young man she so loved with all her heart.

Hannah since the beginning of the second year as a helper had been spending more time at Mr. T's. Her visits were frequent, more frequent than they had agreed to when it all began. She enjoyed the extra employment, but that was not her reason to check on Alfred as repeatedly as she did.

In Patrick's absence, not that his presence could've changed the outcome, circumstance took a grave turn. Alfred was sick, very sick. And even though he was too proud to fully admit it to himself, he

listened and accepted Hannah's every effort to help him. He knew that she knew better than he did, she was a nurse, trained and all after all. But she knew his submission had nothing to do with her being a trained nurse. It's simply that his fear for death far outweighed anything and everything else. Because the fact remained, though blurry to average perception buried deep beneath the pride and the thick layer of sense of humor Alfred was another Patrick Mot, he too was haunted by the irrational fear of death. But who isn't?
Alfred was just as scared of dying as Patrick was. And when Patrick fully told him for the first time about his project, the infinite project, it became the light at the end of his tunnel. No wonder he supported the idea to such extends.

Lung cancer, he only found out a year after Patrick's departure. And it was at a far developed stage, where even a lung transplant would be ineffective - all he could do then was take his prescribed medicine and hope that his body would fight it much longer than the doctors had estimated with the rate of the damage. Yet the former primary school teacher still had hope. Hope that the work of his former prized pupil would save him, cure his illness, cure cancer! But secretly dreaded the lack of time Patrick required to complete his theories and perfect them to application.
Hannah was there - every day, at Mr. T's house, to make sure that he took his daily treatments, ate well and got enough rest. She even at times had to take away the lab keys for Mr. T overworked himself, by spending countless hours in the house lab, and that wasn't good for his current health, he knew it too. But in his defense it sure did beat laying in bed all day dreading the inevitable end when he knew that there was a chance, even as slight as it was, that he could survive this.

There were days were Alfred relapsed, and calling the medical school where Patrick attended made absolute sense to Hannah, but she never did. She would always dial the medical school's telephone number on her cell phone, but would think otherwise about the call before even tapping the call function. Alfred had made clear to her the repercussions of such an action. Patrick would surely drop out of school and rush back home with an idea of saving his life or at the least be by his side when he died. And she would not argue it, for it surely sounded like 'her' Patrick…

June seventh - Saturday morning - Patrick was on his way back to Roseville. Neither Mr. T nor Hannah was aware that Patrick was coming that winter, or any other winter till the completion of his studies for that matter.
The lime green cab, exclusive to the north provinces, dropped him right in front of the gate; he would not get that leisurely walk up the street he's been foreseeing in his head for the last three nights.
With him he carried only his black back pack - inside it was his laptop. He did not bring along any extra clothes other than the ones he was wearing, there were plenty of his clothes in his bedroom.
Inside the house everything looked the same except for the interior wall color, Mr. T had it repainted, and both lab coats were still hanging by the lab door.
There was no one in the house, but he would have caught Hannah had he arrived fifteen minutes earlier.
His bedroom was as he had left it - no one could have entered - only he had its door key which he left with, hence the different wall color from the rest of the house, even the lab Alfred had repainted.
A fresh t-shirt from the wardrobe, but had that stuffy odor, which he masked with a deodorant spray, it was evidence that it had not been worn or washed in years. But it still fitted, though it had been over two years since he had last put it on. And it clearly showed how his body had developed over the years as it fitted a bit tighter around the chest.

In the backroom Alfred laid fast asleep, and Patrick would not disturb his sleep, so he immediately turned back to the house. He'd have to wait much longer to see their reactions to his visit.
After enough TV he struggled to his feet, and stretched his arms wide with a yawn. Still no one had walked through any door. Maybe it was time to see the lab, he figured, there was nothing else to do.
The key to the titanium door was just on the dinner table. Mr. T must have been behaving lately, for Hannah to leave it lying around like that. Patrick reached for the lab coats and hung back Mr. T's after determining which was his. He entered the lab right after putting on the coat which in he looked like a grown up man rather than the young man he was. From behind, at a fair distance, the difference between him and Alfred would be blurred...

At five-thirty that afternoon he walked out the lab and into the kitchen hungry. From the kitchen he could hear the TV and thought that he must have left it ON, but he had not - someone had turned it back ON.

Mr. T must have woken, he reckoned.
As he opened the refrigerator for something to eat, he heard the voice that he hadn't heard in over two years, and it was not Mr. T's. "Alfred! You better had not spent the whole day in the lab or I'll take the key again!" she warned from the TV room.
Patrick still had the lab coat on when she walked into the kitchen. She stood that 'fair distance' from him.
Betrayed by her own eyes she did not realize who it actually was - she thought it was Mr. T for Patrick then had broader shoulders and stood at the same height as his mentor. And to purposely deceive her, he had bowed his head into his chest and raised the collars of his coat to hide the back of his neck, so she would not see that the complexion was not Alfred's. "How long were you in there today?" she asked and quickly warned, "And don't dare lie, Alfred!" her tone sounded familiar, too familiar. A tone far buried deep in his pre and early teenage memories. Somehow in her voice, words and tone alike when she spoke, he could hear his own mother, but he shook away the resemblance as quickly as it came.

He raised his head first, and turned slowly to her. "Hi beautiful!" he greeted with a smile.
Immediately when she realized that it was not Mr. T, but Patrick, she hurriedly approached with a joyous scream and jumped on him.
Patrick caught her, "Whoa! You're heavier." He said looking straight into her beautiful light brown eyes as her lips neared his. And he was right, Hannah had also grown. Her body no longer of a teenage girl, but rather of a young voluptuous woman ready to catch every man's eye who dared to look her way. Nevertheless, the Roseville's upcoming nurse only cared of one man's gaze upon her figure, Patrick's.
"And you're stronger." She noted with her low laugh. It was all thanks to the daily simple fitness exercises Patrick had been doing everyday in the early hours of every morning before class, and later before shower followed by a rather deserved sleep to rest from hours of sitting in lecture halls. And chances were had it not been for those simple daily exercises, he would've failed to lift his own girlfriend in his arms just as he did.
He let her down slowly. They looked into each other's eyes before wrapping their arms around one another and started squeezing tightly while saying how they've missed one another. The embrace was followed by yet another long kiss.

Patrick took off the lab coat and the two stumbled their way into the TV room clutching lustily at each other. They sat next to each other on that 'special couch' and couldn't get their eyes off of one another. In no time, they were once again kissing, gratifying their mutual desires...

Alfred still did not know of Patrick's visit.
When he walked into the living room, Patrick and Hannah were still kissing. "Hannah! What's going on here?" He shouted with a charge at the two, with the full intent to beat up the boy who was kissing with Hannah in his house, but stopped when he realized that it was not just any boy, it was Patrick. "Would you look at what the medical school dragged in!" He was only a step away from the couch that the two sat on.
Patrick was ashamed to greet back.
With no one saying anything Mr. T advised "You two should get a room or something, this is the living room after all." But he quickly advised against it when he came to think of what he was actually encouraging them to do, the meaning that his phrase denoted or rather what it suggested. "When did you get back?" He asked changing the subject.
"A while back, you were sleeping when I got here." Patrick replied "And I didn't want to disturb your beauty sleep, I learnt in medical school that every old man needs it." he mocked with a pinched eye and a smug that Alfred so wanted to wipe off his face.
Alfred knew of Patrick's plan to not return to Roseville till he completed his studies. There was only one thing that could've hurried him back home. She must have told him. So he asked only to confirm what made more sense in his head, "So what brings you here this early? I didn't expect to see you for the next four years, not that I'm complaining, lad." He quickly added "It's good to have you back." and leaned forward to shake his hand. Patrick stood up and instead of a regular handshake he gave the man the shoulder to shoulder tap initiated by a firm handshake. It's incredible how such a simple act can illuminate to the highest degree the mutual respect amongst men.
Alfred paced back to take a seat on the closest free couch and tried to look lively as possible. If Hannah had told Patrick of his condition, he wouldn't want to give him that reason to believe that it was as bad as it actually was. That maybe looking lively rather than a dead man walking would convince Patrick to go back to school.
"Guess I missed you guys." He turned to Hannah to whisper in a different tone than when talking to Mr. T "Mostly you!" and placed his

hand on her thigh, grasping with a firm squeeze, he looked that easily into her eyes and echoed slowly in assurance "Definitely you!" it took everything inside of him to fight the urges to kiss her right then in front of Alfred.
"We should tell him." Hannah spoke evenly to Alfred, and not to ask permission, "He has to know, don't you think?" her gaze had that fiery look, she was young Alice in every way.
"Tell me what?" Patrick asked back, head raised and eyes even at Alfred, "What do I have to know?" he asked again. And in place of interest, concern began to set in.

Mr. T knew exactly what Hannah was talking about, he looked hard at her and said "Hannah is a qualified nurse now." The piercing gaze at Hannah was to strongly suggest that he was against telling Patrick about his cancer, not yet at the least, it had to wait till he finished his studies, should he still be alive by then, which even Mr. T knew was highly unlikely, he'd be long dead then, so he feared.
Unless he completed what he's been working on in the lab, but working on the theory alone without the person who formulated it was like going in circles yet hoping to come across a corner.
Patrick amazed replied "What! That's great! Congratulations!" he wanted to kiss her even more, but he wouldn't in front of him.
"Yes, that's true. I work up at the children's hospital…St. Maps." She was working at same hospital Patrick's mom was working at. Had Patrick told her then that his mother worked there, a lot would've been brought to light, answers to questions Patrick had in the past, the explanation to how she was able to trigger the suppressed memories of his dead mother…

"I wish you could stay longer." He hissed "Much-much longer." silently into her ears, the sun had long set; it was late evening and Alfred had long retired back to his bedroom at the garage.
"I could if you asked nicely." She replied, and didn't have to wait long for his response.
They cuddled on the couch, for both warmth and affection. His manly arms crossing each other on the front of her body, like the safety straps of a race car. His fingers interlocked with hers. Her head planted into his chest, and the hairs on her head smoothly brushing against his lower neck. A movie with a romantic theme playing on the wide screened TV in front of them. It was exactly how she wished it would be when he finally came back home and more.

Patrick lodged his chin into her head, "We never got to do that one thing I wasn't ready for that day we kissed on this couch!" he smoothly reminded.
Knowing exactly what he was talking about she briefly clasped tighter onto his fingers, "I thought you'd never ask!" She whispered back. And for a moment, she could feel the thumbing beats of his racing heart.
"So did I." he said and asked with a whisper "So you wanna do it now?"
"Of course I want to, but we don't have the protection we need for that particular act." Disappointed, she reminded with a laugh and added humorously still "We can't risk having a baby now."
"You mean yet, but I guess we can't." Patrick agreed, and he was as disappointed as she was.
"But..." she began "I think I still have those I went to our old school with, when I went to teach them about protection and stuff." She undid his arms to escape the warming clutches of his person, "I'll be right back." She said, before kissing him and standing up to head for the front door.
"Okay, I'll get the room ready then." He said, and tried his best to hide his over excitement that mixed in with terror.

In what seemed to be the longest fifteen minutes of his life, Hannah walked back through the front door. She had put a pack of condoms in the lady bag she carried with her.
He tried to stand boldly before her, but his knees weakened the moment she got to him, and his lips trembled as he spoke, "You...you have them?" and would only get a nod for an answer.
Their faces only inches apart. Her hands caressing his chest, she shied looking up into his eyes and spoke softly into his chest "I've wanted it to come to this...since that night you held me in your arms for the very first time." she seemed more relaxed than him, her pleasant terrors were well hidden in her beauty. They held hands and walked silently to the bedroom...

It was minutes before ten, when Hannah walked out the room leaving Patrick lying on the bed to go take a shower in the bathroom. She had a midnight shift to get to at the hospital.
After the shower she came to say goodbye to Patrick who was yet to take a shower too. She leaned easily against the door frame and spoke attractively as she looked, "Hey, I've got to go...my ride will be here soon."
"I'll walk you out." Said Patrick getting off the bed, he put on warm

clothes, it would surely be cold outside.
They had both enjoyed their first time together. Yet the two could not find words to say to one another. But true affection can and does exist regardless awkward silence.

He stood behind her, body to body in the biting cold just beyond Mr. T's gate. They stood under the dim light of a street lamppost; the bulb was just too old.
Time and time again he rubbed her upper arms for her warmth. With the freezing cold, it seemed like forever before Hannah's regular ride to the hospital appeared in the distance. They could only see the gleaming lights.
Hannah squirmed round in his arms and stood lightly on her toes to kiss him.
"Is that your ride?" Patrick asked, hoping her answer would be a 'no'. But she said "It is!" when the car halted mere meters from them. A sudden heaviness was upon him, because he wanted to have her in his arms a little bit longer, so did she.
Hesitant but willingly he let her loose, "I hate goodbyes." He said, "Let it be our thing not to say them to each other, ever!"
"Okay!" she said lowly with a smile brightened by the lights of the car before them, "I'll see you tomorrow." she looked that steadily into his eyes and kissed him one last time.
"See you tomorrow." he echoed smoothly, and watched her turn around to walk to the passenger side of the car.
He waited for the car to drive past before turning back inside...

Alfred's house well insulated that even in the cold morning hours Patrick could tolerate the inside cold air enough to walk out the bedroom bare-chested. His skin tightened and lean muscles showing giving him that build of an athlete, like sport was his profession, a track and fielder at heart he would seem like. But he wasn't.
Walking behind the couches to head into the kitchen he could hear her humming, tip toeing he sneaked and as soon as he could see her he'd greet, but with a barrage of questions instead of what one would expect given that standing there before the kitchen counter making breakfast for Alfred was his girlfriend, "How did you get in? I did lock the gate last night, didn't I? You're jumping gates now?" but there was humor in his tone, suggesting that even if the young lady before him had jumped the gate it would not upset or disturb him, nothing about her could ever upset him.

Startled she turned and her heart skipped a bit before melting when her eyes met his exposed upper body as he stood there tall, next to the dinner table in all his half-nakedness, attractively and provocatively like those male models in those cologne adverts, "I work here, Patrick, I look after the old man, remember?" she reminded with a smile. "I have a key to every lock around, except your bedroom…which I'm working on getting, by the way." her smile bright, she slowly approached him. Stood right in front of him, her cold hands instinctively reached for his chest. He shivered. She looked straight up into his eyes and she'd not see a boy, but a man now, her man! "How was your night, love?"
"It was the best I've ever had, and all because of you!" he leaned his head in and pulled it back upright as soon as their lips touched, and continued to say "But after you left…it was very boring I must say."

"But I'm here now." she murmured lowering her pretty eyes, bedazzled still by the man he was.
Standing on her toes she nibbled gently on his left shoulder, gentler so yet he could feel her perfect teeth on his flesh. She slowly slid her hands down from his chest to his bellybutton, where she paused to start navigating the contours of his belly muscles.
Patrick could not ignore, even if he wanted, the effects of what she was doing to him. He gritted his teeth and blew out a current of air still with his jaws locked, he got goose-bumps. Hannah knew what she was doing to him and took pleasure in it. She has been planning this, looked impatiently forward to it, their first foreplay!
"Patrick, I want you again!" she whispered lowering one hand to grab his already fully erect member, "I need you!"
"I want you too!"He said "And I need you more!" he whispered slowly but thickly and pulled on her to hold her body so tightly against his hardened self, his hands pressed heavily on her back. The tables were turned, now it was her under his seduction. His manly hands in a caressing sweep lowered to her buttocks, a sensual maneuver that took her breath and plunged her into the deep ends of her erotic delights. "I want you now!" He repeated thickly and still enforced his masculinity. "I'm so in love with you." He said close to her ear, "I love you, Hannah." He added softly. His dark stature loomed over hers with an intense gaze demanding her response. But she would not say a word. Her head buried in his chest, she dug deep her fingers into his fleshy shoulder blades and just held on without a word still, or any sudden movement.

When she finally dared to look up into his dusted brown eyes, two lonely tears escaped the captivity of her eyes.
Not knowing what to say, or even do, he just held on to her looking down into her shimmering eyes.
Her mouth neared his, and when her lips would gently pry his open he would not offer any resistance.
The moment their lips parted, she spoke softly to him, “Patrick, I love you, so-so much more!”
In a feverish manner he reclaimed her lips and the two would have a stumbling heated *dance* of kissing to Patrick’s bedroom. Alfred would surely wait another hour for his vital breakfast…

Midday, Hannah kissed Patrick ‘see you later’; she wanted her aunt to find her home when she returned from church. And she still had not had her sleep after coming back from her shift.
Patrick and Alfred spent the rest of the day in the lab. They got to talk about why Alfred had been working on ‘first theory’ so much. And he did not lie about his intentions of working on it - he just didn’t make it clear enough for Patrick to get the whole story.
Told the young man that he was working that hard on ‘first theory’ because he thought with it he can cure cancer. The success of ‘first theory’ meant rapid cellular regeneration and rejuvenation. With the complete synthesized serum Alfred could cure cancer. But he intently left out the fact that it was his own cancer he hoped to cure with the boy’s work…

When Patrick left on the fourth of July he was still in the dark about Mr. T’s condition.
Hannah had asked him to buy a cell-phone, so they can keep talking over it. She explained that she couldn’t take missing him, that maybe his voice over the phone would help her deal with his absence till he visits again, hopefully…

Patrick N. Mot completed his medical course towards the end of the year 2024. He would be awarded his medical practicing certificate granting him the full rights to practice medicine.
He had invited both Hannah and Mr. T to the ceremony. Mr. T by then had completed his sentence; he was then free to go wherever he wanted to. The streets of Roseville were once again his to gallivant, so Patrick thought.
On the eve of the ceremony Patrick got a call from his girlfriend. The

call was to notify him that they couldn't come anymore, both of them she said, Mr. T and herself.
When he disappointedly asked why, she did not hide it from him. She told him everything over the phone, she feared that Mr. T did not have that much more strength to fight the cancer that they both have been hiding from him. The sad news left Patrick unshaken, simply because he did not believe that Alfred, his mentor and friend, could be that gravely ill. But this was just his brain playing tricks on him. He simply couldn't imagine the worst of Alfred because he didn't know how to react accordingly to it. We all have it, the coping mechanism.
Patrick the next day after receiving his practicing rights hired a vehicle that would take all of his stuff from where he's been staying during the time of his studies back to Roseville. He did not have that much luggage that would show that he's been living away for about seven years.

He had left Roseville years ago as just Patrick N. Mot, but was then returning with the most envied and a much deserved title added to his name. He was returning as Dr. Patrick N. Mot, MD.

He got back in Roseville in the late afternoon of the twenty first of that December. After getting all his stuff off the hired vehicle and into his room he went straight to Alfred's room, separate from the house. Hannah was seated by Mr. T's bedside when Patrick knocked. She stood to give him a hug. But he just stood there, arms unopened, with his gaze set upon the immobile body of Alfred. And said nothing still when Hannah wrapped her arms around him, she let go and took a step back - she figured that Patrick needed to take it all in first, the critical condition of the man whom took the role of 'dad' when his own father left him in his early teenage years.

The scene was not all that new to him. His father had allowed him countless times into the bedroom he shared with his wife for Patrick to see his ailing mother in her final days.
For a little while there was no exchange of words, just silence in the room, the kind of silence only the scent of death itself had a way of forcefully summoning into existence.
When Hannah saw tears slowly come out of Patrick's eyes down to his chin she got closer to him and said "I know how it feels, but don't blame yourself for not being here." She held Patrick's hand, "There's nothing you could've done, Patrick."
Patrick still with tears slowly streaming out of his eyes began "You

know he's been more of a dad to me since my father left?" He let out a brief sad laugh, "It's funny how now that it's my turn to be more of a son to him he lays dying right before my eyes."
"Patrick, you have been more of a son to him, there hasn't been a day passing where he did not tell me how proud he was of you." She said proud of the man Patrick had become, and she believed it was mostly because of the man who lay dying in front of them. With a smile she added "I even got tired of hearing his countless brags about you at times, you know? I think he'll die at peace and with pride!"
"But he told you...not me." Patrick interjected with a heavy heart. "I want him to tell me himself! I want to hear him say those words to me himself. No! I can't lose him too Please T, wake up, you can't leave me alone, please wake up!" He begged, still with tears flowing like rivers in rainy wet seasons, streaming out his eyes down both cheeks to meet at the base of his chin that he had shaved two days ago in preparation for his certificate awarding ceremony, the salty liquid dripped to the floor below.
"Patrick, I don't think he'll wake up." Said Hannah, she knew and understood the full extent of Alfred's condition, it could only go downhill from then on. "The doctors say there's nothing they can do at this stage of his cancer, and believe me...they have tried everything they know over the years." She did not know what else to say to him.

For a moment again the room was silent with no word uttered.
"That's it...you're right." He began wiping the tears from his face, "They have tried everything they know, but I haven't tried anything I know, I had no say when my mom died nor did I when my father left, but this time around it's different...unlike with my parents...I have a choice, I have a chance. I can't lose him too. No! Not him too, Hannah." he said his heart no longer heavy, he could breathe easily then. He briefly grinned at Alfred "It all makes sense now." he ended with some sort of amusement over his own failure to figure 'it' out sooner.

"What are you talking about, Patrick?" Hannah asked - a bit more confused of her boyfriend's choice of words.
What was he mumbling about? What was it that made sense that she could not see as he did? And what did he mean he had a chance to save him?
"How long can you keep him alive?" he asked with an even face, and if you knew him that well, you'd see in his face that he was standing on an idea. But what was it? Had he learnt something at medical school

that could actually cure Alfred? Had he found a way to cure cancer? Hannah looked that sadly at Mr. T, "It's not me who can…it's his will to keep fighting that can keep him alive." She paused to say "But the doctors with the rate of the cancer's damage to his internal organs estimated that he has a month…or…two, max. Where are you going with this?" she inquired again.
"A month or two, that's all the time I need, to perfect 'it'." He got closer to Mr. T and held on to his lifeless hand, his voice then different from how it sounded minutes ago, "Now I know why you've been working so hard on 'first theory', It's your cancer you've been hoping to cure, isn't it?...Just hang in there a bit longer, okay?" He turned to the confused and concerned girlfriend "We've got to get to work, can you ask for a two months leave from work?" The expression on his face was then the one the girlfriend was most familiar with, but it only muddled her more.
Perplexity evident in her eyes she replied "Yes, but can you please share why?"
"Back in the days when T found out about my idea, he said that he would really like to see me complete it, and that he would even like it more if I tried it on him, I think I'm going to grant him his wish. He's not dying when I can do something about it, for all he did for me, the least I can do is try to give him the one thing no one can, life." He paused, turned again to Mr. T's lifeless body and said "We're bringing Alfred back to life."
She finally caught up to Patrick's plan and began shocked "You mean the lab works? I thought that was just a farfetched but brilliant idea just to pass the time, you actually believe in immortality? You actually think that would really work?" Before Patrick could respond she stated her opinion on the action to be taken at the moment "I think we should leave all this in God's capable hands, don't you?" She did not agree one bit with what Patrick wanted to do, "You don't get to do that. You don't get to turn a man, one you looked up to like a father, into a lab dog. No Patrick!"
Patrick still with his sight fixed on Mr. T replied "When things were in God's capable hands mom died, when things were in God's capable hands my father left, when I left for medical school things were in God's capable hands and when I come back I find T dying…so I think God should really sit this one out." He turned to the door and spoke with his back against her "I'm going to need every file that he's been working on in the lab ever since I've been gone. You can refuse to help

me, I'll still do it. Solitude is an old friend of mine. You of all people should know how best I work on my own. Though I'd prefer doing this with the woman I love by my side, but that choice is not mine to make now, is it?" he walked out the room without waiting to hear what she had to say.

She knew and felt with every fiber in her being that what her boyfriend wanted to do was wrong. But that didn't stop her from following him out, because their love for each other was far stronger than the very concept of right and wrong.

The two, Patrick and Hannah, boyfriend and girlfriend, medical doctor and nurse, worked a whole month straight in the lab without taking a day off. With the young doctor clinging to the desperate hope that he could save the life of the man he looked up to for a father...

A few days into the second month since Patrick's return, when Hannah was tending to Mr. T she came rushing back into the house calling out to Patrick.

Together they rushed back to Mr. T's room.

The machine that measured his vital signs was beeping loudly. It could only mean he was more critical than ever. Patrick looked down at him and said "Hang in there man, we're so nearly there."

"Hannah we have to do it." He added turning his desperate gaze to her beside him "There's no other way and you know it, so please...help me!" he pleaded with her, "You've seen what we've done in the lab, this is the only way to save him, please love!"

Patrick had made clear the two ways to save Mr. T's life to her, but she only accepted one and said no to the other. She had said yes to 'first theory'. Her interpretations of the two theories were simple as black and white. To her 'first theory' was pure genius, and 'second theory' was plain butchery.

The final product of Patrick's 'first theory' was effectively applicable but only to skin and nerve tissues. If he administered serum to Alfred it would do him no good, the serum never proved to work on organ tissues and those were where most of the cancer's damage was. He needed something that could work on his internal organs. Patrick's synthesized serum couldn't do that.

But with 'second theory', Patrick could save Mr. T's life, no doubt about it. In the last month that he and Hannah had been working on both theories they have been able to complete 'second theory' to effective application on two dogs.

Hannah looked at him and once again like before she refused, "I want him to live too Patrick, but that doesn't mean I'm willing to be part of what comes next to have him brought back to health."
"I promise it won't be someone good." He explained, "I'll find the most evil person I can and remove him from this earth. Innocent people die at the hands of these thugs, love. This in a way will help a number of innocent people out there."
"Patrick don't forget that I know you." she began in response, "I know you are not doing this for the innocents out there, you're doing this solely for yourself if not for Alfred as well, but if it will help make this world a better place, a safer place at it, I'll help, but don't get me wrong...I still don't agree with you playing God."
"Thanks love." He got closer to kiss her, but she looked away. He pulled out and said "I knew I could count on you." He turned to the door.
"Where are you going?" She asked.
"The sooner I get the substitute body...the sooner we can begin the procedure and bring him back to life." He smiled, "I miss you, I wanna love you again." A task he admitted to himself the inability to carry out so long as his mentor lied on that death bed. In the last two months Hannah had seen him lose track of time, days even. Sometimes she'd even have to force him out the lab for a shower or a meal. And feared the person she'd have to see Patrick turn into if it all failed in the end. How much will it break him if Alfred died? She wondered in dread.

Three days later, Alfred still remained barely alive, but Patrick had found a perfect way to get David Solomon - the Roseville's infamous criminal that he'd save Mr. T's life with.
David Solomon was the perfect specimen for the procedure he had been not at random selected for. He's medical report confirmed it, plus he was of the same skin tone and height as Mr. T.
After the procedure, should it succeed, no one would recognize that the body was not Mr. T's.
It was four in the morning when Patrick went to sleep in his bedroom after a much deserved quick cold shower in the bathroom, which again left him shivering. But he slept relieved, knowing that he only then had three steps to take to bring Alfred back to life then that he had Alfred's substitute body ready in the house lab. All that was left to do was to decapitate, reattach and resurrect Alfred. No one would bother look for or even report David Solomon a missing person...

The lab works and preparations for Alfred's resurrection were at long last complete. And with the compatible substitute body acquired, at the least, Patrick deserved his eight hour sleep for the first time in two months. But circumstance would not let the young doctor have it.
Just at the crack of dawn, no more than three hours into his sleep, the young nurse he worked with had to come rushing into the house for him.
Hannah slept in her home just across the street, but she made sure that every sunrise she'd walk over to Mr. T's to assess the dying man's condition, and go on to give a report to Patrick in the house, sometimes over joint breakfast.
On his bedroom door she banged loudly and screamed out his name. Yet got no answer back, and when she tested the door, it was locked from the inside. It meant he was in there, and not in the lab, like on most mornings. She could only keep banging and calling out his name with hope that her frail voice at the aid of the bangs would pull him from his slumber.
At only a minute's length Patrick finally came to the door and opened it, but his eyes woke to a sad face flooded with heavy tears. She stepped forward and let herself fall into his bare chest, wrapped her arms around him with a heavy but gentle squeeze.
Patrick was confused as he was surprised, his mouth that close to her ear he asked "What's wrong, love?" but when Hannah looked up into his eyes she couldn't bring herself to it, saying it to him. She could not be the one to tell him the only words that she knew would surely break him, she just couldn't.
After a while trying to calm her down and stop the tears that kept flowing while trying to figure out why she was so sad, he slowly began to see it, just as one would the warm gleaming light from the sun that had been hidden under dark heavy clouds for far too long. The tears were not hers, they were his! She was crying on his behalf.
He held her softly by the shoulders. And when she looked again up into his eyes, Patrick straightened his brow, his eyes widened and he asked with a stutter "Is it... is it Alfred?"The chokes in his voice, she had not said anything, yet he was already shattering.
"I'm sorry!" She said amid her tears, and that's all she said, all she could say really, but it was enough, enough to set him on a rollercoaster of emotions he's never felt the likes of before. He panted heavily for air, and felt himself lose the battle to stand up straight, any moment he would fall down to his knees, it felt. Sounds disappeared. When he'd

look away from her reddened teary eyes everything around him was slowly but surely in his eyes spinning and bending out of shape.
He thought he'd pass out, he hoped to pass out, or at the least wake up on his bed from the nightmare, but he wouldn't, because this was no dream, the moment was as real as it gets. It was the clear and total real manifestation of his worst fear, death, mortality!
And all of the sudden, there it was! The extreme and uncontrollable need to see Alfred, yet he dreaded what he'd see when he gets there. His body told him to step back to take a sit on the bed or even lay back in it, but no, all he wanted was to see his mentor. Stumbling round her he walked out the bedroom barefooted and bare-chested still with only the shorts he always slept in on.
Hannah hesitantly followed after him, walking slowly behind him and unable to stop the loop that played on and on in her head.
That sunrise on her morning routine check-up on Mr. T, she found him not breathing and noticed that the machine that measured his vitals was no longer beeping as it should. Questioning the machines she went on to check the man's vitals herself, the old manual way. With her index finger along with the middle finger she searched for a pulse, and she still reached the same conclusion as the machine.
Mr. Alfred Maoto Tobetsa, Patrick's friend, former primary school teacher, mentor and most of all; father-figure, was no more. He was dead!
His face distorted by the painfully devastating realization Patrick stood looking down at the dead body of Alfred, but his tears, they would not flow, not just yet.

Hesitant at it Hannah finally walked in, and stood closely behind Patrick, who seemed rather collected, shockingly collected.
It was completely silent in the room. Alfred lay dead on the bed and Patrick stood above him like a statue, so much silence with zero movement like the moment itself had frozen in time entirely. Not knowing what to do or say, she just stood there shivering from the nonexistent cold, hoping that Patrick would show some emotion, that maybe that would prompt her of what she was to do next, force any of her natural responses.
And just as the silence and unemotional response started to become concerning to the nurse, it began!
That close to him she could hear his heavy breathing, and just when he would seem to fall to his knees, she quickly caught him only to let him

down slowly. Overwhelmed by the vertigo he held on to the floor and the desperate struggle for air continued. "Hannah! I can't breathe, I can't...I can't breathe!" he said repeatedly clutching his right chest just above where the heart would be. "What's happening to me?" he asked, and with the shock in his voice she could tell that whatever he was feeling he was feeling for the very first time in his life. His heart has never broken before.

"Your heart is breaking." She replied kneeling beside him and turned slightly to pull him gently to herself, "It's pain you're feeling. It will do you no good holding it inside, it's okay to let it out." and like that the bellowing accompanied by streams of tears began and would transition into screams at the top of his lungs. He screamed in cries his mentor's name, begging him to return to the living, begging him to return to him even if it was for a moment to at the least say 'thank you' and even 'goodbye' to those wise fatherly eyes.

Never letting go she held on to him, and that's all she could do for him really, hold him tightly and never let go as his heart broke apart.

Minutes passed and the crying stopped, but to her it had felt to have lasted an eternity. With shimmering wet eyes he looked steadily into hers, "Tell me I made him proud." And at that moment it seemed the right response from her would heal his broken heart or at the least pull the pieces back together and let father time do the rest, mend it.

Her forehead against his and hands on his cheeks she replied truthfully mentioning how Patrick was all Alfred ever spoke of, bragged about even. "And if that's not enough, Patrick, you still have your whole life ahead of you to make him even more proud." She added. And when he would ask her to leave him alone with Alfred and to not call the hearse for the corpse's collection just yet, she would not argue, feeling he deserved all the time he needed to accept what was and let go. She for one knows the dire importance of accepting loss and letting go, three suicide attempts following her own mother's demise...

FINAL CHAPTER: His father's son

'A wise man knows not to fear death, but knows to always be prepared for it, for he understands that it alone is and always will be life's final destination.' said the immortalized Ace.

Mr. T if anything he was prepared for his death and everything that would come after it. He had put everything down to detail in his short and brief will and testament. From the first person to call when he died, all the way to his burial plot and the clothes he wanted to be buried in.

Alfred was one man you'd call a 'popular loner', he knew a lot of people and a lot of people knew him, yet he spent most of his days without them.

The funeral service was well attended. Mostly by teachers from schools he taught in. College friends like Mr. Joel Ossepea and Sir. Jackson were there too, and like the other teachers who knew Patrick they brought along with their condolences congratulations to Patrick's achievement. And his high school teachers were not that surprised to see him and Hannah as a couple.

There were no blood related family members at the service, and that the late Alfred made sure to include in his final requests, that they were never to be sought out or even notified of his passing, yet for pushing him away he had forgiven them all long ago...

It had been three Months since the funeral, but Patrick still worked tirelessly in the house lab.

Hannah kept her daily routine of coming over to the house, but at different times, depending on what time her shifts at the hospital would start or end. Only this time her visits were solely to check on the boyfriend, whom on the outside seemed to be his 'normal' isolated self. But at a close-up look even the half blinded could see it, that he still hadn't let go of Alfred, and seemed he wouldn't. Hannah saw it. Yet on some days he'd seem like a different person, looking forward to tomorrows, but it would not last, every time he'd revert back to his-self.

"I've missed you." He said at first sight, and meant it, "Please stay a little longer today." He added pleadingly and approached with every step firm on the floor but his sight glued with heavy seduction on her beautiful womanly figure.

"I missed you more!" she said as he wrapped his manly strong arms around her, "But I have to go to work, Patrick." And if it were not for the dozen kids who would be depending on her that day, she would have had no problem calling in sick just to spend most of the day with him. "I could come straight here after work, it's a Friday, so maybe even sleep over, if you'd like that."
"'Like that'?" he echoed, "I would love that, almost as much as I love you." and like always using words to reassure each other of their devotion for one another led them to the bedroom.

Already late for her shift she hurried out of Patrick's bedroom and into the bathroom. A quick shower was ought to do it, she figured. But Patrick would join her and only to make her more late than she already was.
Patrick following behind her to the front door reminded her of his lab coat, she was to drop it off at the dry cleaners either before or after work. But she was already late, so she'd definitely drop it off after work.
"There's something inside this one's pocket." Said Hannah with her hand already dipped inside the lab coat's side pocket.
"That's Alfred's coat." He said and anxiously asked "Is it money? An envelope of money? Or maybe a check?" he joked with smiles, sex with her always put him in a good mood.
"It has your name on it." she read the outside of the neatly folded A4 paper and held it out to him, "Open it and find out, but I don't think it's money. And be quick about it, my ride to work will be here any minute now."
Fidgety, he unfolded the page and read it out loud to Hannah whom almost grabbed it from his hesitant hands. '*Patrick, if you're reading this, it means I am dead, I wouldn't let you see this otherwise. This is my only secret.*' It briefly read, and below the phrase an address with a name, of a woman it seemed. And that was it. Yet was enough to plant all kinds of thoughts in his head You could see in his face that he couldn't wait to head out to where the address led.
"Good luck solving the mystery, wish I could join you, but some of us got jobs." Sarcasm! "Who knows, maybe Alfred had daughter." She hurried out, and even had to run a little for the driver of the car outside had had to hit the hooter twice already...

Patrick had to call a taxi to the house for his trip, and in that moment getting a driver's license began to make more sense. But the concept of

driving still did not fascinate him.
After one hour thirty minutes in the back seat of a cab the taxi drove through a town. And something about that town as they passed through it, felt very familiar to Patrick, as if he had been in the town before. And the truth was he had, but was too young for the memory to have taken proper hold.
He had requested the to-and-fro option when he called the taxi, and mentioned that the distance time might extend to hours.

When the driver stopped the taxi and told Patrick that they had arrived it was in front of tall gates of a research facility he's never heard of before. But he heard the likeliest reason Alfred would send him to such a place. The infinite project, maybe there he'd meet someone who can help him finish it, perfect it. But he believed to have already perfected it to application.
After dropping Patrick at the gate, Rabi, the cab driver told him that he'd rush into town to fill up the tank, that he'd not take more than ten minutes and he'd be back at the same gate to wait for him...

"Here goes everything." He said to himself and headed for the security checkpoint at the gate. Fitted with a visitor's tag he was pointed to the main building's entrance. Once inside he'd have no idea of where to find the mystery person. But if he could find the reception area the name he had with him would be enough information to find the person if they worked there.
The whole building itself was a maze, that every new employee was ought to get lost one too many times in their first week. But the reception area was the one department that was made easy to find. Greeted by two friendly ladies he began "I'm looking for..." before he could finish his eyes beat him to it by reading the name card on one of the two ladies' uniform that he had to end by saying "I'm looking for you." instead.
The discovery was a disappointment. Why would he be sent to find a receptionist? But buried deep within it was yet another mystery for him to solve.
"One Alfred Maoto Tobetsa sent me, apparently to find you." He explained and was surprised when the receptionist replied to say that she expected him a lot sooner, even called him by names, first and last. "Follow me, and it's Dr. Mot now, right?" she inquired and when Patrick affirmed puzzled still by what was happening, the lady slowed her pace to add, "This is unbelievable! You really are his son, and not

forgetting to mention becoming the one thing he tried his best to keep you away from. Now that's something."
Trying to speak above the sound of her high heeled shoes he replied coming to walk slowly beside her "Well, Alfred was actually the one who pushed me towards becoming a medical doctor."
"Who said I'm talking about Alfred?" she asked and pointed to the last door on their right, "He's in there. Oh! He doesn't know about this, so he might react not as you'd expect."

Before he could ask 'who was in there?' he heard first the distinct voice, it was one of the few voices he'd never mistaken for another. Hesitantly approaching the door he came to stand before it already turned inward. And there he was! But he looked a lot older than he remembered him. He had aged, but it was still him right there, his father, John Mot, in the flesh. Presenting to his colleagues a new procedure for genetic alteration that may results in selective mutations.
Catching a figure at the corner of his eye John paused and turned to the door.
The receptionist expected a happy father and son reunion, but stood corrected when Patrick scowled and frowned with a burning stare at the old man before turning away without a word. One foot in front of the other he walked a little faster than he did when he walked in. What Alfred and Bridget had planned and foresaw to be a happy reunion turned out to be the opposite.
"He just got out!" said Bridget to John as he paced past the reception area looking for his son. But he was too late, or is there such a thing? Either way, Patrick was already inside the cab when his father came rushing to the gate with his lab coat flying and catching the wind behind him.

Two hundred meters from the gates, in a four way intersection, just when Rabi waited for the green signal light Patrick prompted "Please turn back!" and repeated "Turn back to the research facility, it's okay, I'll pay for the extra drive." And Rabi would not hesitate to do so, as soon as it was safe to make the u-turn he did.

John stood hands at his hips in the middle of the parking lot when the taxi pulled over before the high massive gates.
Looking at him as one would a high school teacher he did not like but was forced to talk to he approached just after asking Rabi to not drive

away.
Standing before his father he would not say the first word, even preferred to say no word at all.
John had aged, it showed, patches of grey hair on his head and the beard on his chin was completely grey, but his build was bold and looked stronger than most his age "Hi, son." The father greeted. But the son would not greet back! The lead research scientist could see in the eyes of the young doctor before him the anger and hostility that burnt in them towards him. He knew the words that would come out of his son's mouth should he speak would not be pleasant to the ears, but he would not hold them against him. Whatever ill mannered response Patrick would give john felt he deserved.
"You have grown." Began the seemingly proud father, "Alfred told me about your studies, you must be a doctor by now, how's the old man doing anyway?" he asked, and it revealed he knew not of Alfred's passing, probably didn't even know about the cancer.
"Yes I'm a doctor now…but I'm not here to talk about that, or talk about Alfred." He spoke at last "He says his only secret is here, I doubt he meant you're here…there must be more to it, but if that's all his secret is, tell me so I can leave already." He ended, and he would not it from him, the scowl with the piercing gaze that said he detested sight of his own father before him.

"Son, I…" John would not get to finish.
"Don't do that!" Patrick interrupted only to warn his father with uplifted emotions, unlike with Mr. T he would not bother to mask his anger "Don't dare call me that again, you do it again I'll turn and walk away. It's just Patrick, just Patrick Mot to you. Only Alfred gets to call me that. So what am I doing here?"
"I deserve that." He agreed and continued, "I guess my whereabouts are the secret. Son, Alfred has always known where I have been all along from the beginning."
When he spoke with drawn brows, his father felt every ounce of his disappointment "A mistake is thinking I was Joking." He said, "You don't get to call me 'son'. That address is no longer yours to place upon me." And just like that Patrick turned to walk away, and never turned even once to his father who kept calling out to him…

Hannah on her way back from work bought a few groceries for him. In the kitchen already she sounded her loud 'hello'. Coming to her in the kitchen she was met with a gaze she knew too well. Something had to

be wrong, she suspected. His trip must have not been exciting as they thought it would be.
"Hey, what is it? What was he keeping from you?" she asked first, "Is it that bad? You look...'like yourself' right now." she added and wrapped her arms around his neck, she searchingly looked up into his eyes and stood on her toes to kiss him when she would not find what she was looking for in them, a clue to his current state of mind.

"It's my father." He began looking easily back into her eyes, "Alfred has always known where he was. I met with him today."
"That's great, Patrick! So why don't you look happy?" she just had to ask, "I would have loved to have been there with you to meet him."
"It's actually for the best." He said, "Wouldn't want you to see the person the sight of him turned me into. What's to eat?" he asked approaching the fridge and swung open its door with no specific item in mind.

Shocked she had to ask back "Aren't you gonna talk about this?" she followed closely behind him round the kitchen, "Patrick, you just saw your father for the first time in over ten years, you have to talk about it." she advised.
He paused his search for food, and she could tell he was thinking, but what about, she could not tell. "I'm going to bed, please lock up when you leave." He requested, "I don't feel so good." He ended and turned to leave the kitchen.
"I'm staying tonight." She said lightly, "Are you eating first or taking a shower first?" she asked.
"I said I'm going to bed. And you're leaving." He stressed and his voice intensified, "It will do you good to stay away from me right now." he had stopped walking.
Quickly she replied "What about you? Will it do you any good to be alone right now?" when he answered to say 'of course not.' She added quickly "Then I'm not leaving. I'll go ready that shower." She said, but Patrick would not let her walk passed. From a hand reaches away he grabbed her hand and pulled her to himself.
"Move in with me." he said with a deep low voice that gave her the chills down her spine. Stunned by the request she feared to look into his eyes. She had expected him to say something else, maybe even argue the matter of staying when he strongly suggested that she should leave. "Did you hear me?" he asked when she seemed to have not heard him, but she did. Yet would not respond, she just looked back at him as

if looking through him like a transparent glass. "Say something!" he urged her on.

Finally her lips moved, "Patrick I want to move in with you, but I think you're only asking me now because of what happened today." She said looking admiringly into his dusty brown eyes, "Decisions born of temporal emotions are often regretted, ask me again in two weeks and I'll gladly move in, in fact I would love to move in with you." But when his head moved closer to hers and he looked that deeply into her eyes every fiber of her being wanted to say yes. And if only Patrick asked again she would have not suggested otherwise.
"Okay, two weeks." He agreed and asked "So what do you wanna know about today?"
Feeling his breath warmly on her cheeks as he spoke that close to her she kissed him first, "Everything, love, obviously!" she said, and Patrick pulled her into the TV room by the hand. When he sat on the couch opposite the TV and her on his laps he told her everything, from the moment he got into the cab all the way to how his father called out to him as he rudely walked away. Even told her the taxi driver's name and how he was able to impressively tell that Patrick was a doctor by just looking at him, he relayed the conversations he had with the driver along the drive, no detail left out.
He looked back into her eyes and could see how she thought he should have stayed a little longer to hear his father out. That maybe all the old man wanted was a chance at redemption. And if Hannah had maybe told Patrick that maybe his happy reunion with his father was what Alfred wanted for him, maybe he would reconsider his decision of never wanting to see his own father again.

"That Man left me at the age of fourteen, with nothing but proof of my names and a journal I was too young to even understand." Said Patrick evenly, "I'm even thankful for it, him leaving me I mean, I got to live with Alfred and fell in love with the smart and most beautiful woman I know. As far as I'm concerned Alfred is my father." He added and swiftly pushed her to stand before she could even ask him why he never spoke of Alfred in past tenses, like how all the dead are supposed to be spoken of. Not even once he'd talk of him in past tenses, like he refused to accept that he was gone.

When he said there was something he needed to do in the lab, that he'd be in and out, Hannah refused to let go. She knew very well how

Patrick tended to lose track of time in there. And it would be no use to try and pull him out for he locked the door every time. And knocking or calling didn't work on that room, she knew that too well, yet still tried it sometimes.
"I promise, all my work in there is done now, I'll be in and out." he repeated , and when he pressed her gently against his hardening self she looked up into his eyes and balanced on her toes to kiss him. With loving eyes looking down into hers he added "Go draw us a bath, I'll join you in five minutes, I promise, five minutes."
Over the trousers she held on softly yet most provocatively to the half erect member, still looked that steadily into his dusty brown eyes "Five minutes and not a second more, Patrick." She said, and it sounded more like a warning rather than an invite for him to come and have some adult time with her in the bathroom.
Patrick moved further away in reverse with his gaze upon her face still and smiled as she made the words 'I love you' silently to him.
Love struck he entered the lab and would still lock the door behind him on instinct...

From deep within the thick walls of the bathroom she could hear the faint knocks.
Wiping her fingers that dripped of warm water from testing the temperature of the drawn bath she walked out the bathroom to investigate. And when she probed for a name the voice on the other side she could not mistaken for another. She opened the door more to confirm than to invite him in. And indeed it was him, her uncle.

"Seanokeng! Afternoon! You don't live here, do you?" the man asked already suspecting in dread the one reason her niece could be there in that house, the young man who lived in there, "What are you doing in Alfred's house, Seanokeng?" he called her by her middle name, always.
"Remember years ago I told you I was working as a house keeper to pay for nursing studies?" she reminded, "This is 'where'. How did you even know Alfred?" she asked, "And I leave over there, uncle." She pointed out her house just across the street. Right there right then the man standing before knew! He knew that his attempt had failed, there was no way her niece could have not yet met the young man who lived in that house with Alfred, maybe they were even friends he thought, or worse!
"I'm friend with the old man, can you please call him out for me." he requested, "I haven't heard from him in months." But his thoughts

would not abandon the idea that her nice had met the young man who lived with Alfred.
"You didn't know?" she sounded surprised and equally sad for her uncle whom just revealed that he's friends with Alfred.
"Know what?" her uncle asked, "Did he move away?"

"No." she said and paused before adding "Uncle, Alfred passed away three months ago."
"That's impossible." He said in disbelief, "I was with...the young man who lives with him just earlier today. He said nothing and spoke of him as if he was still alive. Is he in the house, Pete? Can you please call him out." he asked concerned of the young man's well being.
"He does that." She said, "I guess I have a weird boyfriend. He's locked away in..." he would not let her finish.
"Seanokeng, your what?" he sounded his disapproval and invited himself in, "Not him, Seanokeng. No!" he said and stumbled to the dinner table, nearly fell to the floor, but managed just in time to grab the chair and pulled it to sit. It was worse, the two had not just met, the two were not just friends, the two were lovers!
"I'm old enough to decide for myself, uncle." She responded, "And why not 'him'? What do you know about him?" she asked.
But she would not get words for a reply, only tears that dripped fast onto the vanished table surface as her uncle gazed hard into it with his fist clenched hard close apart on the table.

Standing opposite him on the other side of the table she could not understand what was going on that she had to ask "Uncle! What's wrong?"
When the fifty four year old raised his face tor her, he revealed a side of him she's never witnessed before. But Patrick on the other hand had seen it all before. After all, he was old enough when his mother died for the events of that day to take proper hold in his memories.
"I didn't know." The uncle spoke amid his tears, "I didn't know it was Patrick whenever you spoke about him in the hospital. That's why I didn't feel the need to interfere, Seanokeng, You deserved at the least happiness. How could I have not known you lived so close to him."
"What are you talking about, uncle?" she asked still confused.
"Your death is going to break him." he replied wiping the tears from his cheeks and drying his eyes, they were dusty brown just like Patrick's.
"But aren't we all going to die in the end?" she asked not knowing

where her uncle was going with this conversation and his disapprovals of the man she dated.

"Yes we are." He acknowledged, sticking that nose that resembled Patrick's in every way in the air. "But you, Seanokeng, a lot sooner than most. And if he loves you like you've revealed he does every time you talked about him to me, it will break him. Your death will break him past repair." He added, his face dry and its even toned dark complexion untainted by the salty tears. A true older version of Patrick Mot he was, how could she have not seen it herself? All these years, and all these clues! She still remained blind to it.
"Uncle John what do you mean?" she asked, concern settled in.
"I'm sorry, Seanokeng." He began, "Worrying would have robbed you of your happiness. I didn't see the point in telling you something you couldn't do anything about, especially if that thing would have only made you sad." He paused "Seanokeng, you have the same virus my Alice had." He revealed and went on "You got it that day they had to use her blood to save your live, they couldn't see it in the test because not much was known about it yet. I've been working for twelve years now and I'm still no closer to a cure, I can't save you. But you can save him, by staying away from him." he ended.

Reduced to tears she stood there looking back at him, but she would not panic, quite the opposite actually it would reveal as she spoke, "It's okay!" she said "I'm grateful for what Aunt Alice did for me. Every day I wake up knowing today is a gift, so if I died tomorrow, I'll say I had more than enough. But I'll be sorry for the ones I love and have to leave behind. Especially 'him'." she smiled genuinely, "My death is something I can't control, and his hurt from it will be an equally unwanted result. But the sorrow after my death will only prove how much he loved and cared for me too. I will not purposely hurt him by walking out when he needs me most. His father did that to him already. That is what will break him beyond repair." She ended drying her own tears. "But I have to ask, why do you care so much about him, uncle, you know him?"
"Remember when Alice and I offered to adopt you, you said yes and we said 'we'd have to talk to our son about it first before we talked to your family'?" He reminded, "Well...that's him, that's our son. Seanokeng, I'm Patrick's father!" he revealed evenly just like how Patrick would have.

It amused her that she laughed, but jolted her to her feet in disbelief as she began to see how the face of the man before her began to similarly

resemble that of the young man she loved with all her heart.
"No way!" she said standing a few steps from the table but her eyes fixed on those across the table still. "You can't be! You shouldn't be! His father is supposed to be this evil man who left him with nothing and nowhere to go to. It can't be you, Uncle John." She refused to believe.
"That's not entirely true." said her uncle slash father of her boyfriend "I did leave Patrick, that part is true. I only did it because I knew for certain I wasn't fit to raise him anymore with how I was when his mother died. But I made sure, Seanokeng, I made sure that he had a place to go to with everything he needed and someone to keep an eye on him. That was Alfred. He knew about my plan from the beginning, I actually considered sending Pete to a boarding school like I told you I had all these years but he suggested otherwise, said I should leave him with someone he wouldn't be afraid to be his true self around. We both knew when Pete discovered my disappearance he'd go to the one place he knew to be his second home, right here. Alfred even talked me out of coming back when he got sent to prison." He explained and Hannah hated that it made total sense. "Had his mother not gotten sick that early, you and him would be brother and sister! I guess in a way you two were destined to be in each other's lives."

"Then why do you disapprove of me being with him?" she asked "If we're so destined to be with each other."
"Because, Seanokeng, he's just like me. He did not know what I did for a living but he still turned exactly into it, a medical doctor through and through, hell bent on curing the incurable just like I am." he said, "He's controlling, possessive, cares too much, blames himself for everything that goes wrong around him and worst of it all he bottles up his pain till it's too much to bare and he implodes. Yet he hides it all so well, but I'm sure you've noticed some indicators though." He ended.
"No." she said and defended "He's not like that at all." Yet she knew it was all true, he was all that. And you wouldn't have to look far to support that given the events during Alfred's critical days, the lengths he went to. He abducted a man, drug dealer or not, it's still criminal, yet to him it was nothing.

"Where is he even?" the concerned father asked, "We need to talk to him about all this and hear what he decides." But he already knew what his Pete would decide given the revelation. He would try and want to save her life. Maybe the son could succeed where the father has been failing for over a decade.

“He’s right in there.” She pointed to the titanium door “It’s his lab. He should be out by now. He keeps the door locked so I don’t disturb. But I see it as more of saving him from overworking himself on a rather farfetched idea than disturbing him.” She approached the door thinking the father would ask of the farfetched idea. But John already knew, Alfred had told him of his son’s work from the first day he himself found out about the project.

Any minute now he’d come out, she hoped. And she instinctively tested the door, it miraculously opened.

She pushed it slowly and as soon as the crack was wide enough she got in and pushed it close behind her. A thick semi-transparent plastic zipper curtain divided the room into two. *“This is new.”* She thought and slowly approached the divider.

Slowly undoing the Zipper she got through and right there before her there he was. Lying on a lab table turned into a hospital bed with white sheets. He breathed slowly and peacefully like the constant beeping sound of the heart monitor hooked to his body was his perfect lullaby.

Hannah’s heart slowly pounded hard against her chest, making her feel every heartbeat. The beeping sound of the EKG machine flooded her ears blocking out all other sounds, but when Patrick who had actually stepped out of the house to the backyard moments ago opened the door behind her she heard, yet remained frozen in disbelieve of the face she looked down upon like she was seeing a ghost!

Seeing her figure through the divider he spoke softly while walking over side by side with his father, “Hannah! This is not how I wanted you to find out. I was going to tell you once he woke.” he said and that’s all she heard. Because the moment Patrick crossed through the divider Hannah losing her balance to stand straight searchingly swung her hand round for him and when she held on to him she turned, looked into his face and began to faint slowly. But had enough strength left in her to speak as she looked up into his worrying eyes, “So your parents are John and Alice Mot, how wonderful!” she spoke slowly and she would have to ask “Patrick! How is he…How is he still alive?” Her beautiful eyes had closed and her grip on him began to loosen, she asked again when she went unanswered the first time, “How is…how is Alfred…still alive?” she easily passed out, lost consciousness right there in his arms…

This is merely the end of the beginning.

After all, death does come in threes, always! And it shall too for Patrick Mot. His mother first, who shall be next? Who shall be second, since old man Alfred still remains among the living. And finally; who will he lose third and last? His girlfriend whom he loves so much is likely to make it into the list given the 'virus' she carries. Ponder these questions and possibilities for Patrick Mot too shall complete his circle of loss. Just like his own father before him, John Mot, who lost his mother, father and lastly the one true love of his life, his wife, Patrick's mother. It comes in threes, always…

www.ingramcontent.com/pod-product-compliance
Lightning Source LLC
LaVergne TN
LVHW080847170826
845678LV00006B/1739

* 9 7 9 8 8 4 6 7 8 7 3 9 1 *